DANCING WITH MAHARAJA

— in the IAS exam gullies

DANCING WITH MAHARAJA

– in the IAS exam gullies

Sundar

Srishti
PUBLISHERS & DISTRIBUTORS

Srishti Publishers & Distributors
N-16, C. R. Park
New Delhi 110 019
srishtipublishers@gmail.com

First published by Srishti Publishers & Distributors in 2012

2nd impression, 2012
ALL MAJOR CHARACTERS IN THIS NOVEL ARE 100% FICTITIOUS ANY RESEMBLANCE TO ANYONE LIVING, DEAD OR TO BE BORN IS PURELY COINCIDENTAL

Typeset in AGaramond 12pt. by Suresh Kumar Sharma at Srishti

Printed and bound in India

To all the IAS aspirants

To my brother –

for introducing me to the world of civil services

Acknowledgements

Sitting inside a lonely forest bungalow nestled in the tusker areas of Hosur, I did not even dream of seeing my story as a book. I just kept typing pages and pages of connected words. But today, we are *Dancing with Maharaja*. I am lucky enough to have dozens of friends, philosophers and guides (!) without whom those words would not have turned into a book.

Lots of thanks to Meena, Venkat, Muthuvel, Siva, and comedian Praveen Kumar for their constant support. They have been there for me – for over a dozen years now. I am grateful to my friends from bureaucracy – Anish Rajan, Anandhi, RV Karnan, KL Nanthakumar, Abdul Hakeem, and Prashanth N – who ensured that I kept going. Special thanks to Anandhi, Anish cheta, Karnan, Padma Rajeshwari and my cousin Brindha for their time, motivation and big help with the story. Nantha and Mayur Bhuva, my Symbi room-mate, need a special mention for keeping me ticking.

Many thanks to Sandeep Misra and Shiv Kumar Rai for getting me started with publishing. But for their help this book would have been just lying in my laptop as one bulky word file. I am grateful to Dipin Ambalia and Ashok Chandran, for their timely gyan on publishing. Big thanks to my cousins Shrinath (KT) and Satish Kumar, machan Jay, friends Janakiraman, Solaisamy, Sridhar Dora, Rahul Dora, K Sreedhar, Ravi, Sivaraj and Meiarul – for their overall support and solid help with the cover page designs. Thanks to Jack for my photo. Unlimited thanks to Manimaran and Viyan Aarman for giving me this cover design.

Special thanks to Smarak Swain – for his attitude, energy, ideas and above all – for introducing Srishti Publications. Smarak, a big thanks to you buddy – without you this would not have been possible. I am grateful to Bose*da*, for believing in me and helping me out throughout the production process.

My sincere thanks to Sh. Mukul Pathak, psychology teacher at Vajiram & Ravi, for making me see a new world; to my IRS seniors Sh. Sunil Chander Sharma and Smt. S. Padmaja for their time and motivation; and my chitappa Sh.Krishnamurthy for his constant encouragement.

Jeyanth, my best buddy since our school days, deserves a special credit. Without him, I am not complete. Though no words can justify, I owe everything to my parents – for giving me the life I have now. Finally, the biggest "thanks!" is to Jayanthi – my wife. Her contribution to this book is matchless.

Sundar

Panaji

01.01.2012

PART I: ROLLING STONE

It was like a *mela*. Only the illuminated giant wheels and pink cotton candies were missing. Amidst the sea of unshaven young men and anxious ladies there were active islands of media persons and uniformed men. They all were on a wait. Some eager; some tensed; some hopeless; some helpless. Some were there just on duty. Many had waited for this day for about a year; Many others for years together. The next few minutes would decide their destiny; would decide if they had instantaneously turned famous and powerful or they would have to go through the same year-long ordeal again or worse if they had been pushed out of the IAS race forever. This was also the day when the tea shops and the chat-*walas* in that area did their peak sales. But this was an annual ritual here.

9th May 2001. Dholpur House. Shahjahan Road, New Delhi.

Office of the Union Public Service Commission (UPSC) of India.

It was 4:30 in the evening. 10:30 AM was the expected time. "This always happens!" a balding person near the outside notice board was obviously annoyed. His friend looked calm. He offered his half-smoked cigarette and said philosophically, "We have been waiting for years… do these extra hours really make a difference?" "How do you feel? Do you think you will get a rank?", adjusting her microphone, a young reporter asked one of the better looking candidates in the tea shop. She was almost thrusting the mic into the person's mouth. The apprentice camera man was trying to get the frame right. The person took time and replied, "I hope I get something this time"; He resumed sipping the steaming brownish liquid that was passed in the name of tea. It would be out any moment. The results of the Civil Services Exam conducted by the UPSC, popularly called the IAS Exams, for the year 2000, would be put on the two huge notice boards – one inside the premises and the other one outside. Those sheets of computer print outs meant a lot to those who waited there; also to the hundreds of IAS coaching centres across the country, the candidates and their parents, grandparents, wives, husbands, distant relatives, friends, fiancées, bosses, children, landlords, pet dogs and many such groups. Rajaraman was also one of them. Every passing minute took him to a new level of restlessness. His heart was pumping as if there was no tomorrow. For a moment something within told him that his son, Satish, would emerge as Shri.R.Satish IAS; the very next moment the same thing mocked at him. How foolish it was for him to expect Satish, who had taken five years even to get an engineering degree, would make it to the IAS. Unable to handle his record anxiety Rajaraman had returned home around 3PM leaving the affairs of his Maharaja Wines near the Madurai main bus-stand to Satish.

"I will let you know *pa*...I will get a call...in any case it will be out before six", Satish told Rajaraman before seeing him off. Looking cool Satish was chatting with one of the customers while the store boy was taking out a chilled Kalyani Black Label.

Summer. 1992. Satish was in his X standard. "Satish cleared his class VI only with grace marks... you know that", "Have you ever seen him take even a newspaper in his hand?!", "I know what all he does in his school...Horrible!". "You are a liquor shop owner...don't forget it...and IAS is not for students like Satish." The last statement was from Rajaraman's best friend, and like many others he too genuinely felt Rajaraman was just kidding them or was having momentary fits of insanity whenever he spoke of his dream of making his son "R.Satish I.A.S.". But no matter what others said, Rajaraman did not give up a bit on his crazy dream of seeing his only son as an IAS officer. He tried out all the tricks to somehow turn his son into a top-notch bureaucrat, specifically – the District Collector, Madurai.

"You should also do something for the country...society" Rajaraman opened the conversation with the then schoolboy Satish on their way back from Maniratnam's *Roja*. Satish nodded dutifully. Satish loved our country as much as any other kid. But he did not exactly understand why his father was lecturing him about serving the society etc. He was also puzzled why his father was talking about making him an "officer" when it should have been quite natural for him to take over the liquor business. "No stops for the bottles" Satish often told himself. He also loved the fact that even on days like 2nd October, Maharaja continued with its huge sales – secretly from an Omni van parked across the road. A thousand kingfishers happily danced in Satish's dreams.

"I spend 80% per cent of my time behind this one boy and only the remaining for all other 1000 students". The headmaster of Prime Higher Secondary School, Madurai was under severe Satish-induced stress. He requested, ordered, pleaded and even cried to get Rajaraman put his son in a different school for Classes XI and XII. In the bargain Rajaraman got the headmaster mark "Excellent" in his son's conduct certificate.

It was the time when the entire district was gearing up for the inter-school, senior-level, cricket tournament. Students from class VII to X were eligible to be in the teams. The Prime team was handpicked by the headmaster (HM). Though he generally went by the performance of the students in the school-level games, recommendation too worked at times. Kumar, Satish's best friend, was the captain of the team. "Let him not be in the playing eleven sir…but please keep him in the team. He is an asset for us…", Kumar ensured that Satish also found a place in the school team.

A month of rigorous practice began. The coaching camp started at 5:30 in the morning with a few warm up exercises including three rounds of the school ground. The PT master took charge of the fitness sessions and as someone who had opened his college's innings during his better days, he took special care of the batsmen. There was a bowling coach, imported from Madras. His one-point agenda was to turn the tenth class kids into Kapil Devs. The training plan was to have a short practice match on every third day during the camp. Satish attended the camp only during these days. He was made to bat only at seven down – if needed. He never bowled a single ball. He was generally given a fielding spot where the chance of a ball being hit was zero. But at the end of the session Satish always took extra eggs and two glasses of milk. Fearing Satish would finish off dozens of eggs Kumar often had to remind him, "Probably those who played also need them..." The rigour of the camp increased with every day. The inaugural match was only a week away. The Prime boys were resolved to get back the trophy they lost the previous year to their arch rival – Government Boys' High School. "Boys…you will bring back our lost glory…", the HM pepped up the boys who were drenched in sweat. He dropped in for the last two days of the coaching sessions. He did not seem to worry about Satish who had missed the session even on that day.

The tournament started. Prime was racing through the league matches. So was the Government School. A line on their team's progress was mentioned in their respective morning-prayer assemblies. Just after the Government School had won the seniors' trophy the earlier year, their Principal had quipped, "You should play against our junior team….you might win." The ego of Prime School's HM was yet to recover from that punch. He did not want to compromise on anything during this tournament. Among other things he ensured that the kids were given eggs and glasses of milk during the training. Earlier, something in between water and lemon juice used to be served.

It was not difficult to guess that these two schools would meet in the final match. Till then Prime had lost only one league match in the tournament. The team had a rhythm. But the position of the Government School was not encouraging. Though it had won the semifinal – it was only by sheer luck. Only a mere two-run margin landed them for the final against Prime. The Government boys were not mentally prepared to challenge their arch rival in the final. It was under this circumstance that the Government Boys' High School headmaster gave the go-ahead to win the finals against Prime – by any means.

The mood in the Prime camp was upbeat, naturally. Kumar was also in great form. But for his trips to the pitch with the water bottles, Satish had spent most of his time in the dressing room.

The final match. The Deputy Mayor, Madurai Municipal Corporation, in a white dhoti and a matching half shirt, tossed a 1-rupee coin. "Head." Kumar called it right. Government team made 134 for six in the 20-over match. "We have won bigger matches. Just focus on the game." the PT master patted Kumar. The captain confidently walked in to open the innings. Things were okay till the end of fifth over. Score – 28 for no loss. Both the schools had gathered a huge crowd for the match. The district stadium was charged as if it was an Indo-Pak match. Sixth over. Kumar facing the ball. But he was looking uneasy. The wicket keeper was murmuring something from behind. Kumar was 34 not out, but he struggled to concentrate. End of ten overs. The keeper's nasty words were getting at Kumar. Sledging seemed to work well for the bowling team. Kumar was trying to remain calm; but was losing focus. Score – 63 for 4. Break time. Satish ran towards Kumar with a bottle of glucose-water. "Any problem?" Satish asked him. "Nothing.", Kumar returned the bottle after taking two sips. The crowd got noisier after every ball.

Two fours in a row, one caught behind, one run out, some smart singles, many runs and five overs later. 111 for 6.

Kumar was at 44. Just ten runs from him in the last five overs bowled. Occasionally he had replied to the keeper's comments. The opponent captain and two others in the slips had also joined the keeper with their low-voiced abuses. Last four overs. 24 runs to win. Four wickets in hand.

The students of the rival groups were booing at each other. Kumar seemed to say something to Satish, who had again gone with the glucose bottles. Some tiny stones and chalk pieces were being hurled at the opposite camps in the crowd. The teachers did not bother much to control these missiles. The match resumed. The noise got louder.

Three more overs bowled. Two more wickets down. Fifteen runs scored. Kumar playing at 48. He had scored just 14 runs in the last eight overs. Nine runs needed from the last 12 balls. The Prime HM secretly started chewing his finger nails.

19th over, first ball. A single and Kumar got the strike. 8 more runs from 11 balls. Kumar missed the next three consecutive balls. 8 runs needed, 8 balls to be bowled. Kumar tried to pull the next ball, but got hit on his ribs. The crowd roared. The Government boys booed. One group of the Government boys shouted, "East or West". The other set responded, equally loudly, "Prime is the worst!" Kumar took time to collect himself and got ready for the next ball and knocked it hard. But he could manage only a single. Just two runs from the 19th over. The HM was giving up.

20th Over. Kumar was away from a 50 by only one run. Prime were away from the trophy by seven runs. Six more balls to go.

Kumar missed the first two balls. The Government School crowd started dancing and whistling. They raised their voice and shouted in chorus, "Down, down…Prime!" Many students started making fun of the Prime HM, who had started to chew nails openly. He also shouted restlessly, "Come on! Go for it!"

The pieces of chalk and stone missiles were growing larger in size.

7 runs needed from the final 4 balls. Satish was looking calm. Kumar was ready for the third ball. It was a low level full toss. Nobody could believe what they saw. The coach and the PT master buried their heads in their palms. On any other day even Satish could have hit that for a four. But now the ball had gone like a rocket and had broken the middle stick into two pieces. Kumar stood there like a statue for a moment, turned back and stared angrily at the wicket keeper and the fellow in slip; he started walking out dejectedly as he had let the whole world down.

It was then out of nowhere Satish jumped and ran towards the pitch. He was holding a huge, red parcel in his hands. Before anyone could grasp what was going on he had reached the centre of the pitch – and lighted the 10,000-wala crackers. "Cheats!! Bastards!!!" One could not hear exactly how his abuses progressed as the 10,000-wala was turning the ground into a war zone filled with noise, smoke and loads of cracker-confetti. The rival students got on the pitch to exchange blows; they were armed with bats and wickets. One of them threw the cricket ball at the HM. It did not miss the top of his head. The lesser mortals limited themselves to throwing small stones and similar rockets at the opposite gang. The teachers and the Deputy Mayor madly ran for cover.

The last three balls of the tournament were never bowled.

Satish proved he was an asset to the school team.

Rajaraman started taking Atenolol after that cricket match a year back. His blood pressure lowered; but his mad dream of seeing his hopeless son as the Madurai Collector grew bigger.

"Look Satish…you will be finishing your school…in a year. Have you decided what to do after that?" Satish's father was a little hesitant yet optimistic, when he used "in a year".

"Yes pa...I will do B.E."

"After that..?"

"What do you mean? I will take over the crown from you...Maharaja is waiting for me..no?"

"Liquor shop after engineering?! Well... okay, but what about the IAS Exam?" his father politely asked. Satish gave a blank look and continued to sip coffee while gazing at the latest heroine import to Kollywood posing in a black swimwear. His father softly pulled the newspaper from him, "Why don't you understand? You will have a great life, excellent life...everyone will respect you – wherever you go. You can't command that kind of respect in any other profession...even that of..." Satish abruptly stopped him. He was tired of hearing that same lecture over one hundred times during the last few years; and ran out of patience this time. "Then why don't YOU write the exam?" he shouted and walked out of the room, banging the coffee cup on the table. Rajaraman disappointedly glanced at the big, garlanded photo of his wife that was hanging on the wall to his right.

At the Maharaja Wines bar that night. "My uncle was just a clerk at the tehsildar office, still people gave him more respect than what my father got...though my father was earning in thousands – even in those days...in thousands. Money cannot really get everything...", Rajaraman zealously continued after a brief pause, "I want my son to be respected, I want him... to be on newspaper, on TV. I want him to control many people…I want him to have power… I want him to be a success in life." Rajaraman was with one of his close friends. Rajaraman was holding a tea cup, while his friend was taking frequent sips from a Bullet bottle. The friend was patiently listening to that flashback for the hundredth time. Rajaraman persisted with that story for a while before ending with, "I will definitely make my son an IAS officer...district collector...Madurai Collector." His friend too gave his usual response packaged with a deep laugh, "Even if heavens fall, that will not happen!"

Thomson effect, Wheatstone's bridge, Rayleigh-Jeans law, Huygen's principle, Kirchoff's law and many more. Physics paper, TN Higher Secondary Board exams, 1994. It was the last paper. Last paper of Satish's school life. Like many other exams this particular exam was also faultlessly designed to test a student's memory power. Satish's interest in physics was limited only to the apple that fell down. Gravitation, induction, refraction, diffraction – everything meant the same – nothing – to him. However, similar to other exams in the past Satish was well-prepared that day also. Their team of four boys was in place. Two were sitting to his right side across the walking space and one was just in front. They had short-listed five out of twelve chapters in their physics book. These priority five chapters were enough to make them scrape through. Each of the boys had prepared one chapter, with Satish doing an extra chapter. They had put in lots of efforts in preparing for the exam – in their own way.

Tiny pieces of paper, geometry-box bottoms, big white erasers, wooden one-foot Camlin rulers, the bellies of the exam hall desks and even a corner of the black board in the exam hall – nothing was free from tiny inscriptions of intimidating formulas and crisp code words. Depending on the location, the inscriptions were with black ball pens or white chalk or pencils. For these four, taking the physics exam was like conducting an orchestra – demanding high skill-levels, perfect timing, and outstanding coordination. Even a slight slip in the timing would leave their future jeopardised. However, Team Satish was confident that, being the last day the hall supervisor would be lenient with them.

The last thirty minutes of the exam. Satish was waiting for the big eraser to reach him. It was to fly across the walking space from his comrade's seat on the other side. The eraser had a few circuit diagrams and some mind-boggling equations with Greek alphabets sketched on it. But the invigilator did not turn out to be an easy-going one; he was like a short-stringed pendulum in that narrow, walking space – taking quick-paced walks to and fro. Probably he was expecting to get a pat from his boss by trapping students like Satish, red-handed.

Looking at the invigilator's movement the partner across the path had to abandon the circuit diagram launch twice. Satish was getting restless.

The last fifteen minutes of his school life. Unless that eraser reached him that moment Satish would not be in an engineering college the next year; worse, he would be appearing in the same physics exam the following year too. Satish did not particularly worry about an extra year, but was really terrified by the idea of taking the physics paper again. "I should not see these formulas again!"

He pressed the emergency button – he coughed thrice.

The hall supervisor looked at him and continued with his walk, up and down the path. He did not infer anything peculiar with those deep coughs. But he became more suspicious. Exactly a minute later the sharp alarm from a digital wrist watch disturbed everyone in the hall. *Beep. Beep. Beep.* It was from a student sitting in the opposite corner of the hall. He was apparently struggling to stop the alarm. It seemed because of that exam-tension he was not promptly able to stop the alarm of his watch. "What is that?" shouted the supervisor, and rushed towards that corner. "Er…Sorry sir…alarm…last fifteen minutes…sorry sir", the student apologised as he finally stumbled on the way to turn off the alarm. The supervisor had reached that corner. He stood there looking down at that student for shattering the focus of all other serious exam-takers.

It happened in the meantime. The big eraser with those scary equations and the terrifying circuits successfully landed on Satish's desk. Satish's school life too ended successfully. "No more laws and formulas."

Rajaraman was happy that his son was expecting to clear the Class XII exam with flying colours; Satish was hoping to manage a pass mark in all the papers. There was a period of about two months for the results to be out. Rajaraman decided it was the best time to inspire his son and make his life turn towards IAS. His earlier efforts like lecturing about the powers of a District Collector, showing patriotic films, reading news items on successful IAS officers etc, all have failed. In fact those efforts have failed so miserably that instead of making Satish develop an interest in the career, they gradually made him even more allergic to the three letters – I, A and S. So Rajaraman decided of something that would definitely mould the tender heart of his teenage son.

"Satish… be at the collector office at 3:30 today."

"Why?"

"I want you to meet the collector. 3:30. Collectorate. See you there."

"What?!"

"Just shut up and be there. I have a meeting with the collector at 3:30. I will request him to see you after that...he is a nice man. I will leave home early... I have some other work before the meeting" said Satish's father, who was also the president, Madurai Wine Shop Owners' Association.

Language was no bar to Satish when it came to watching good movies. He was glued to the pirated video tape of *1942: A love story* till 2:30. He then put off the Solidaire TV and the VCR. He was normal till that point. However, when he started to get ready for the Collectorate, a strange feeling of fear gripped him. So far he had been ignoring the thing called "IAS". He just had a vague idea that a District Collector was someone who – traveled by Ambassador with a red beacon on top; was always accompanied by a coterie; inaugurated schools and bus-stands; inspected PDS shops and PHCs; distributed prizes and old age pensions after the Independence Day parade; held frequent press meets and gave interviews on AIR; called on the ministers and important politicians whenever they came to the district; was also transferred at will. But now when Satish was supposed to meet the Collector himself in an hour, he was simply feeling strange. "Who gave this crazy idea to my dad?! Is he joking?" He went to the terrace of their bungalow and took a puff from the cigarette that was hidden in an abandoned, unfinished room. He was not sure how he was supposed to get dressed – did it have to be formal or casual dress would do? Finally settling for a pair of dark blue jeans and a black full sleeved shirt, he left for the Collectorate after wearing a pair of new looking sneakers.

It was 3 PM when he reached the Collectorate gates. Everything seemed new to him this time. People stood in groups under the shade of huge neem and tamarind trees that dotted the campus haphazardly. There was a congregation near the tea stall which also served packed lunch and snacks, a few white Ambassadors and many Mahindra jeeps. He could see some old women with one of the younger ones having a badly injured child in her hand, robust men dressed neatly in spotless white dhotis and whiter half sleeved shirts, dozens of college students with registers and placards in their hands, a few police constables and an SI standing by the police jeeps, a young boy selling newspapers and magazines, two advocates in black coats surrounded by a mob, the parking over-flowing with hundreds of bicycles, scooters and a few brand new Hero Honda bikes, some old men discussing politics over glasses of tea and a few government jeeps pouring in and out of the campus.

There was nothing new to him; but he felt as if he was seeing all this for the first time in his life. He was anxious, for no apparent reasons. Slowly he walked towards the office building. "Am I really going to meet the District Collector?" He was not able to come to terms with the fact that he would be face to face with the Collector.

He spat out the Wrigley's Spearmint in the unused dustbin, and started going up the stairs. The Collector's chamber was on the third floor. On the first two floors Satish again saw groups of men and women waiting outside some chambers and a few peons in white uniform moving from one cabin to the other either with files or cups of tea. For a moment he thought the place resembled a market or a busy bus stand. "What are all these people doing here!" There was a huge display panel with the vital statistics of the district and some messages like *Say no to child labour*, *Save rain water* etc. He was about to go up the stairs to the third floor, when someone called him out. "Brother!" It was a girl in her early teens. She continued, pointing to the row of chairs on the other side of the corridor, "I have come with my grandma…I need a help from you brother". Satish instinctively nodded and asked her what the matter was. "We have been waiting here since morning 11:30…to meet this officer", she showed Satish a chit of paper. "We have not received any compensation from the EB department…my father died seven months back while repairing a street light. My grandma only takes care of me and someone had told her to meet the Collector." Satish listened carefully, though he had no clue why the girl had chosen him. Trying to maintain her calm the girl continued, "We had come here at around 10 in the morning but the peon in Collector's office asked us to meet this officer… but this officer is yet to call us in. I don't know what to do… " Satish stood there quite perplexed and helpless. He was already in a state of confusion, and this EB compensation problem added to it. He thought for a while and asked the girl to write down the details and give him. "I don't know…but…I shall try, okay…take care", said Satish before going up the stairs.

On the third floor he could see the Collector's chamber and the adjoining meeting room in the other corner. There was a huge crowd in the nearby waiting area. Luckily, in no time Satish located Rajaraman. He sighed and walked towards his father hiding any sign of anxiety. There were a few, huge framed photographs of leaders like Gandhi, Ambedkar and the former Chief Ministers of Tamil Nadu on the sides of the corridor. His father smiled at Satish and said matter-of-factly, "Meetings got delayed today". "We were given the sixth slot of the day, but only the fourth meeting is going on now. So far the review of the education department, EB and PWD are over. DRDA is inside…the Additional Collector sir is inside", Rajaraman, proudly told Satish, as if he were the P.A. to the District Collector. Satish was quite irritated by his father's recital of the Collector's timetable. In the meantime, a few people rushed out of the chamber and went back with some more files in their hands. One of them took in two cups of tea and some biscuits on a tray. "What can we do about this?" Satish showed the chit the girl had given him. "Keep it...let us see", Rajaraman said after listening to the story behind the chit. The father and the son waited for more than one hour. Around 5 o'clock the Dean, Madurai Medical College, entered the room with a few doctors. From time to time the Collector's staff asked the crowd outside the room to keep quiet. "Agriculture, SC/ST welfare and transport meetings are after ours…looks like one of them is going to get postponed", Rajaraman told Satish. Satish was getting ready for the meeting with the District Collector, Madurai. He went to the wash room, came back looking fresh in. He had a sip of water from the almost-defunct water cooler that was by the staircase. His father and a few others were also waiting to be called in any moment. The group of doctors came out at 6:30 pm. The group of trade body representatives including Rajaraman entered the meeting room. "Just remain here", Rajaraman told Satish before going in. Satish was as nervous as if he were appearing for an interview for the first time. "What is happening to me? Come on…be cool", he told himself.

The place was still abuzz with people running around with files. It was around 7:45pm when Rajaraman came out of the meeting room quickly and excitedly. The other members of the meeting were coming out slowly. "Come on!" Rajaraman hurriedly told Satish while forcibly pulling him into the chamber. Satish's heartbeat was racing. Even before he could realise what was happening he was inside the meeting room, face to face with the District Collector, Madurai. Satish trembled for unknown reasons. He had seen the District Collector on the television earlier but it was the first time he was seeing the actual man. He felt strange. Somehow Satish managed to greet the Collector, "Good morning…er…good evening sir". Middle-aged. Striped shirt. Looking somewhat tired. The trousers were hidden behind the huge oval shaped table with tiny microphones placed corresponding to each chair. The District Collector nodded and asked, "How are you doing?" And without waiting for a reply he continued, "Your father said your aim is to become an IAS officer…my best wishes!" Satish was completely caught off guard; but somehow collected himself to utter, "Sir…er…no…yes sir...thank you sir…sir." "Thank you very much sir, we will take leave now, sir," Satish's father said cheerfully and even before Satish could realise what was happening he was outside the meeting room, face to face with his father.

Satish's heart was trying to slow down. But it was still beating very loudly. Satish was full of anger for his father, who had put him in such a fix. But Rajaraman was looking happy as if his son had already become an IAS officer. "Well done Satish", for no reason Rajaraman patted Satish while getting out of the room. Satish did not feel like uttering a single word to his father. "This man is mad... Why should he say such a thing to the Collector!", Satish told to himself. Suddenly Satish remembered something and without bothering to think even for a moment, he entered the meeting room again and directly went to the Collector, who was engrossed in some pages of hand-written notes. "Sir...can you please do something about this?", Satish asked politely while handing out the chit given by the girl. In the meantime the Collector's P.A. had come to him. The Collector looked at the P.A., who by then had already snatched the chit from Satish. "Sir...I have already got the details in the morning… I will get it done sir", the P.A. told the Collector while giving a not-so-kind look at Satish. Not very convinced, the Collector asked the P.A. what it was about. But Satish chipped in out of turn and started, "Sir…I will tell you" and narrated the episode as told by the girl. "Please help her sir." The Collector said in a reassuring tone "Hmm... I have about four hundred petitions pending…" and looking at his P.A., "Why is the delay? Ask the EB SE to meet me tomorrow." Satish felt satisfied. "Thank you very much sir."

"What happened? Why did you go in?" an intrigued Rajaraman asked Satish. Though Satish was in a good mood, his anger for his father had not subsided. He did not answer Rajaraman's question. They were coming down the stairs. Only after reaching the ground floor Satish opened his mouth to ask, "What is wrong with you.. why have you become a 420?" he asked furiously. "Forget that! Are you not inspired now? Look, how powerful the Collector is!" Rajaraman shot back and waited to hear encouraging words from his son. Satish contained his anger and said, "Yes! Amazing!" and pointed towards the Collector's car that was parked outside and

asked "But why is he still traveling by this old, horrible Ambassador?"

Like many other dull sons of extra-rich men in Madurai, Satish also landed in the notorious EC Engineering College in the city. But unlike most others he took an extra year to complete the four-year course. Kumar also found a place in the same college. They were in the computer science engineering department. They were the founders of the seven-member college gang, The Desperados.

It happened in his third year, 1997. There was a box item in two local newspapers that while exciting a few angered most in the city of Madurai. It went like this –

INVITATION: *EC Engineering College is proud to announce the screening of the super-hit English film, family entertainer, Basic Instinct today in the college auditorium at 7:00 PM. All, especially aspiring software engineers, are cordially invited!*

It was like any other first day of the month of April – pranks aplenty. But The Desperados wanted to make it big and probably stretched it too far. By noon the ad had created a ruckus in the entire town, and to an extent in the whole state. Within a week, there were even news items in a few magazines on the falling discipline levels of the college students. All such articles invariably pointed to this incident. The Desperados were pinned down. A meeting was called by the college management, The Desperados and their parents were summoned. Mr.Sakthivel, the director-owner of the college was waiting to pulverise this bunch headed by Satish; copies of the newspapers and magazines, with the box item visible, were lying scattered on the big, round teak table; a few fathers with heads hung down in shame and with their sons near them; others were waiting to kill their kids before they reached home after the meeting; the attendant outside the meeting room was waiting for a chance to peep in – he expected a lot of action. Kumar looked nervous. Other Desperados were looking either at the marble flooring or the former President of India Shri.Radhakrishnan's photo that hung in a corner of the room.

Satish did not look ruffled, but was dead inside – not because he might be kicked out of the college, but because he could see tears in his father's eyes. Satish also knew everyone in the room would have noted the moist eyes of his father. Unlike the usual "union is strength" philosophy of such rogue groups The Desperados had a strange don't-go-down-as-a-group policy. They felt that it was foolish to go down all at a time. Whenever there was a scene like this, one of them became the scapegoat, by turns. This turn system had its own advantages. Once a person takes the blame, the issue would be put to rest by the crowd and that made it easier for the other Desperados to regroup and bail out the scapegoat. It was their philosophy. Further the turn system was cast in stone among The Desperados and it had never happened that someone had dodged from taking the post of a scapegoat. Satish was lucky; Kumar was not. It was Kumar's turn this time. But Satish somehow felt that this crisis needed his sacrifice, as it was essentially he who had thought this bright idea for the April fool's day. In fact he wanted the film to be *Kama Sutra*, and it was only after Kumar's intervention that was toned down to *Basic Instinct*. He fought and convinced the other Desperados to make him the scapegoat. Kumar did everything to prevent this but ultimately the leader's veto power prevailed. Thus Satish ended up getting an out-of-turn appointment as the scapegoat.

On any other day, such a "crime" would have called an immediate dismissal from the college and possibly some court cases too. Rajaraman had to fall flat at the director's feet to get the dismissal of his son reduced to just a one-month suspension. He also had to shell out a lot of cash as fine. After getting back from the college he did not speak even a word to anyone, including the servants.

That night, while drinking alone on the terrace of their bungalow *Satish villa* in the heart of the city, Rajaraman felt a slight pain in his chest.

Monsoon. 1998. With the results of his final semester exams in July, Satish had created a record of sorts in his college for failing to clear the first year mathematics paper – even after taking it for seven times. Satish somehow was not able to achieve the feat of clearing the paper in spite of his best efforts and innovative exam-hall strategies. He and Kumar had also taken an agent's help in tracking down and taking care of the evaluator. But even the deadly combination of a few thousand rupees and carefully chosen Scotch bottles could not deliver the passing marks to Satish. *The Desperados* minus Satish got the BE certificate.

He initially even tried to be sincere and attended the first-year mathematics classes again. But soon he realised sitting in the lecture halls filled with juniors was not a very good idea and instead he decided to join some private coaching. But for the one or two hours a week that he spent at the coaching, Satish spent all his time on things that came to him naturally, like – picking up silly quarrels in cinema halls, watching cricket matches and drinking at the end of every match immaterial of who won, assembling near tourist spots to catch glimpses of the out station female crowd, relishing street fights with other groups of equally jobless youth, playing gully cricket and repeating the events that happened during the finals of the tournament in his class X, and during one of their frequent trips to the Kodai Hills even giving in to the vice of highest order.

However the other *Desperados* in addition to all the routine ventures were also helping out their fathers in different kinds of business that ranged from construction works to manufacturing safety pins to leather tanning to running theatres. Kumar was assisting his father with the truck rental business. Satish too had plans to expand the business of Maharaja Wines, as he was sure this was one of the few businesses that never had any lean period. "Success or failure everyone wanted a drink", he told himself often. He clubbed all his plans and dreams for the liquor shop under the vision "Maharaja 2005". By the year 2005 he wished to see a transformed Maharaja that included a one-of-its-kind high class bar-cum-discotheque in Madurai city. Satish also nurtured a secret, wild dream of replacing his idol, Vijay Mallya one day, as the most famous face of the liquor industry in India. "Maharaja Breweries...no Satish Liquors...mmm.. no it should be Madurai High..", very often Satish confused himself with the probable names for the liquor empire he dreamt to create. It was also around this time Kajol impressed Satish. *"Kuchuu kuchhu hota*...what?", asked Satish with a confused look. Though he had seen a few Bollywood movies, all he that knew about Hindi was – it was a language spoken by many people near Delhi. Anyway by then he was already curious about this film that had reached far south, even without being dubbed into Tamil. Earlier it was *Hum Aapke Hain Kaun.* "Don't struggle with the title! My Hyderabad cousin was crazy about this film...let us also give it a shot", Kumar's words landed them in the last row of *Maapillai Vinayagar* cinema hall that evening.

Australia lifting the cricket world cup was still fresh in everyone's memory. July, 1999. Satish had also managed to win something that was as tough as winning the world cup for him. He had finally cleared his first year maths paper. He achieved this result with the concerted efforts of various stake-holders like the exam hall invigilator, neighbouring candidates, college staff and the evaluator. It was a true team work. Now, Satish was a computer science engineering graduate; a free bird. Armed with a BE certificate Satish planned to take over the operations of Maharaja Wines. His Maharaja 2005 vision was growing. By now Satish was also thoroughly convinced that taxes on liquor production and sales were forming a major part of a state government's revenue and it was his moral duty as a responsible citizen to contribute to this revenue stream of the government. Though over many years Rajaraman had untiringly lectured and told Satish about the status and power of an IAS officer, the latter was not even one per cent interested in the IAS. He felt the career took fun out of life and gave back only a few things in the name of status and power. "More than anything else, how could this man even think that I can sit and prepare for the IAS Exam! He needs a psycho doctor", Satish felt pity for his father. Also Satish's idea of social service was limited to helping and bailing out any Desperado in need, sponsoring booze parties on a monthly basis and organising blood donation camps on the days around the release of a Rajni movie.

Satish planned to learn the liquor stores business hands-on for a year and then work towards his vision of Maharaja 2005. Till then Rajaraman had somehow managed to keep Satish out of the shop mainly by harping that Satish could not enter the shop as long as he was a student. But now he was no more a student, he was a full-fledged computer science engineer. "There is no way he can stop me. I shall learn the nuts and bolts of the business first and then work towards my dream", Satish was determined. Other than Maharaja Wines, Satish did not find anything else exciting in life. However, ever since the days of *Jurassic Park* during his class XI, Satish had developed a soft corner for computer graphics; and *Titanic* impressed him so much that he joined a 3-D animation course at Pentamedia during the third year of engineering. He had also used his computer classes to design a logo for the liquor shop. The logo had a crown that resembled the popular version of Alexander, the Great's crown – imposing style, metallic in colour with attractive red feathers on the top. "Maharaja" was inscribed in Gothic below the crown. Satish also frequently talked about his ideas and dreams for Maharaja Wines and how he wished to fly greater heights. The Desperados were really surprised by all this. They did not know even Satish could be serious about something in life.

Rajaraman too was getting serious with his plans for his son. He was up-to-date regarding the IAS Exams and the coaching classes. He had about two more months to pack his son and send him to Delhi for the coaching classes that started in the first half of October. The preliminary exam would be in the following year, 2000, in the month of May. He had heard that New Delhi was the best place to prepare for this exam, and he somehow wanted to pack his son off to Delhi. Now Satish and his father were waiting for each other to make the first move. Satish wanted his father to open the topic of IAS preparation; his father was waiting for him to open the topic of Maharaja. The month of July passed like this.

Satish's father did not seem to initiate anything. Satish too gave a tough fight but ultimately ran out of patience, mainly because he found the other desperados getting busier with their respective business, and he was getting bored to death.

He decided to start.

But suddenly he realised that if by some miracle his father agreed to transfer the responsibility of the shop to him immediately, he would have to get disciplined in life from that very moment itself – getting up on time, wearing neat clothes and abandoning wrinkled t-shirts and lungis, keeping track of stock, manning the shop and managing the men, bargaining with the dealers, ensuring the quality of supply, handling cash, keeping away quarrels near the shop, dealing with policemen and managing the government, renewing the licence, attending the association meetings, missing cricket matches on TV, staying away from films on first days, handling politicians during rallies and meetings and missing the Desperados. So he decided to postpone the talk with his father and carried on with his routine of sleeping, drinking, eating, quarrelling etc for a couple of days more.

August 16, 1999. Satish had fixed this as the date for starting career related talks with his father. It was his mother's birth anniversary. He thought of a plan – he would be up at 6:30 in the morning as a sincere, responsible man, do some exercises in the hall of the house so that his father could notice him and be there at Maharaja at 10:00 AM sharp, dressed up neatly. That would be about 30 minutes before his father reached the shop. He also planned to visit the nearby Murugan temple on the way, just to impress his father with *Prasadam;* The Desperados too gave a green signal to the plan. They were somewhat convinced that by now Satish's father would have lost hope in making his son prepare for the IAS Exam and given Satish's vision for Maharaja, the best option he had was to induct his son in the liquor business.

The day arrived. Satish was up at 6:30 AM as per plan. Around 7 he walked briskly towards the hall and started with a few stretching exercises. His father was having a cup of filter coffee; he was looking calm. Satish shifted gears and managed some push-ups; topped up with more vigorous exercises. At the end of 40 minutes Satish was drenched in his sweat. He had not done any such thing in his recent or distant memory. He remembered those good old days when he used to skip the cricket training sessions, when all his friends were struggling. He glanced at the direction of his father, who seemed to be deeply engrossed in the pages of national politics in the newspaper.

No reaction from his father as yet. Satish took a bottle of ice cold water from the fridge and joined his dad.

"What's the news pa?"

"You are the news, my boy!! What has happened to my dear, useless son...you found your *bodhi* tree?!" – This is what Satish expected his father to ask him. But he was stumped when his father added – "Nothing new...the usual murders, robbery, rapes, elections etc..."

Satish, without showing disappointment and left with no other choice, Satish talked animatedly about weather, Kargil, cricket, corruption, computers etc. His father too responded eagerly without showing any kind of surprise at seeing an apparently transformed Satish. That drama continued for another 20 minutes before ending with the topic of the newly introduced semi-sleeper deluxe buses between Madurai and Chennai. Satish was totally frustrated – not even once did his dad bring up the topic on the new, enlightened Satish. "Anyway he will be surprised to see me at Maharaja today; I hope I can convince him then."

Satish got back to his room confidently. By 9 AM, the otherwise usual time of his deep sleep, he was neatly dressed and waiting for breakfast at the dining table. His father joined him without showing an iota of surprise. Eleven *idlis* and three cups of *chutney* later their conversation was still at the oncoming general elections in September. By then Satish was thoroughly irritated. "Why is this man behaving strangely today?!" At his father's suggestion they prayed in silence for a minute, in memory of Satish's mother. Satish cooled down. But the next moment itself he thought it was the limit and almost opened the topic, however he waited to surprise his father at the shop. His father was as calm as if it were any other day. Satish was dying with restlessness.

It was 9:25 AM. Satish entered his room to pick up the keys of his bike. He noticed something on his table when he was just about to leave his room. He picked it curiously – it was a railway ticket with the details – Train no.2621, Tamil Nadu Express, Boarding at Madras, Reservation upto New Delhi, M 22, AC 3-tier, 2200 hrs, 02-10-1999. For a moment he could not make out what it was about. Once he realised what it meant he did not know how to react. He was speechless, thoughtless, and emotionless. He was staring at the ticket; he went through the details about half a dozen times. No change; he had got the details right even at the first go. He could not believe his own eyes; he could not understand what was happening. The long key chain of the bike was dangling from his index finger that together with the thumb was holding the ticket. Suddenly the sound of his father's car leaving the bungalow shook him and brought him to his senses.

Satish quickly ran out calling his father; Rajaraman's white Cielo was too fast to wait for Satish's angry and loud voice.

Satish zoomed to Maharaja Wines in his bike. He did not go to the temple on the way. "Your father is at the bar", said the store-boy. Satish entered the bar, agitated. Rajaraman was calm. There was no one else in the bar that was well-lit with green tube lights and some white and red, zero-watt bulbs. Customers would start coming only around noon.

"Why this kolaveri dad?" Satish shouted taking the ticket out of his pocket.

"I do not want you in this shop."

"I can't be an IAS officer."

"Well… even I don't want you to be one." Rajaraman replied coolly.

"What?!" Satish asked, baffled.

"Yes…I am not totally off my mind to dream that you will become an IAS officer…also you have great plans for Maharaja…" his father paused.

"So?" asked Satish while crumpling the railway ticket.

"I want you to prove to me that you can be disciplined in life…", and Rajaraman continued, "I just want you to go to Delhi and prepare for the IAS Exam."

Satish was completely taken aback by his father's reply, "Have you gone mad, dad? I do not see any logic…I can be disciplined even here…", Satish raised his voice and added, "like today."

"You need not. Just do as I ask you to. You may takeover this shop form me – only after writing the IAS Exam. You prepare well. Write the exams."

"But..this is…" Satish interrupted. Rajaraman gestured him to keep shut and continued, "…Come back and take charge of the business. Buy, sell, destroy, build, eat, drink. Do whatever you want to do…but only after writing the exams."

"Senseless…mad!"

Rajaraman started in his usual calm style, "That's how it is. I'm not even bothered about your results. I just want you to appear in the exams," but topped it with an angry voice, "Is it asking for too much?"

Satish was upset beyond words with his father's plan. He was highly disappointed to see how wrong his father's thought process could get; he still could not come to terms with what he had heard. "Is IAS Exam like an entrance test for Maharaja Wines?? Hopeless idea! People will laugh if I say this! And come on dad…you know my capacity to sit and study…" Satish tried to get the logic from his father.

"You have about fifty days to leave. Be happy at home eating or with your bunch of rogue fellows or whatever till then. You may go now… Just visit the Murugan temple on the way back."

Satish spent his last days in Madurai – partly as a zombie, partly as a thrilled soul. The mere thought that he was going to be away from his friends and the associated activities gave him deep sadness. He would be missing every lane and by lane in the temple town. But occasionally in some corner of his heart, he also felt that the IAS Exam-Maharaja Wines deal was not that bad and he could have some fun in Delhi before taking the huge responsibility of running the liquor shop. He did not want to disappoint his father all the time.

It was the night before Satish's north-bound mission to enjoy Delhi life. The Desperados were hosting a farewell party for their leader.

"Toast to our Collector, Mr.R.Satish I.A.S.", the other Desperados cheered while holding a transparent, disposable cup of beer or brandy, based on their capacity and liking. Kumar's voice was the loudest and naughtiest.

"Don't spoil my mood you morons!! I want to be free from this IAS-virus at least for the next one hour", he shot back.

"Ok Collector sir!!" the others said in unison like little kids reciting nursery rhymes. A mixture of the sound different kinds of laughter followed it.

Three hours. Eight bottles of Kalyani, one half-bottle of Old Monk, one full-bottle of Honey-bee, a few plates of scrambled eggs, lots of cigarettes and a dozen packs of Malabar masala chips.

Satish spoke while opening the ninth Kalyani, "My dear… darlings! I have a request for all of you...please tell me...please…where is the mental hospital? Mental hospital..."

"Why? Do we get free liquor there?" hyenas laughed.

"Ssshh..I want to admit that old man, that owner of Maharaja Wines. Can a sane man even think of sending someone like me to Delhi, that too for this Iiiii.Aaa.Ssss. Exam? Me-IAS…egg-jam! No…I need to admit him…him...now. Mental hospital, where?"

One more hour. More solids, liquids and gases.

"Where is Arnold? Where is the Terminator? Call him right here…shoot Thiruuu.R.Rajaraman."

Back at *Satish Villa,* Mr.R.Rajaraman was busy finalising the travel and stay arrangements for his son.

Rajaraman was waiting at the Madras Central railway station to see his son off. The train was about to leave in ten minutes. They had not talked much since the time they left Madurai for Madras in a super deluxe bus. After filling his son's bag with stuff like Bisleri bottle, *Mysore pak* from Adyar Anandh Bhavan, a pack of Krackjack biscuits and a few bananas, Rajaraman opened the talk, "Try to be at least 1 % per cent sincere with your preparation, I will be happy." Satish nodded while looking at the railway signal on the other side.

The train squeaked. Satish was on the footboard looking at his father. Rajaraman waved his hand. No words. Not even a single tear drop. But both of them were feeling as if they had lost everything in their lives.

PART II: LION CAGE

October 4, 1999. Congested roads capable of confusing every new visitor; filthy service lanes needing immediate helping of bleaching powder and phenyl; college students with coloured hair and ear studs; air filled with the aura of *tandoori kebabs* and chicken Manchurian; underweight rickshawalas bargaining for extra two rupees; unrelenting women in bright sarees refusing to give even a paisa more; internet centres with bright boards saying Per hour Rs.25 only; a few nameless and homeless souls called beggars; school girls in red skirts, white shirts and bags over-flowing with text books; property agents having a field day before the start of the IAS coaching class season; old couples left to themselves in some equally old houses; the green-yellow auto rickshaws finding their way through the maze; the ever-crowded Mother Dairy outlets; the Blueline buses plying carelessly on roads oozing with people; pigeons flying in sync, suddenly; colourful *shamianas* and loudspeakers across the roads getting ready for some late night functions; healthy rhesus monkey families terrorising everyone else; puny children delivering hot tea and *matri* for the nearby shopkeepers and IAS aspirants; the gigantic, blue room coolers lying idle in the balconies; homeless construction workers making *rotis* inside the unfinished multi-storied apartments; the juice shop attracting students throughout the day and night; a few hefty police constables roaming around in heftier bikes; 4-foot kids delivering 20-litre Bisleri cans in their bicycles; macho men in tight white t-shirts and faded dark jeans; a group of foreigners outside the tourist information centres and nearby hotels; cloth banners, with names of coaching institutes, tied across the lamp-posts of crowded streets – that is how the Mecca of IAS preparation – Old Rajinder Nagar, New Delhi – welcomed Satish.

Satish booked a room in Hotel Royal Prince in one of those countless by-lanes of Old Rajinder Nagar. He availed the 20% discount that the customers got when they do not ask for the receipt. After freshening up he decided to meet a guy named Mohit Swain.

Rajaraman had got Mohit's contact after a lot of ground work. Mohit had been in Delhi for four years; preparing and appearing in the IAS Exams. He also took some classes at Achieve IAS Coaching (AIC) – the most popular IAS coaching institute in the area.

Satish had a strange feeling when he stepped out of the hotel. "What is all this IAS preparation stuff happening in my life?!" He was confused. He reminded himself that it was going to be just a long vacation for him in Delhi – nothing to do with keeping awake the whole night, going through bulky books on irrelevant subjects and appearing in model tests. He glanced philosophically at the liquor shop that was just opposite Royal Prince. It was overflowing with people of all age groups and to his total surprise he saw many customers walking away with liquor bottles – without the customary wrapping of newspapers or black polythene.

He added one more point to Maharaja 2005 – a branch at Old Rajinder Nagar.

Now Satish had the arduous task of locating Mohit's apartment and seeking his advice – on managing life in Delhi amidst the language problem; and the Exam-related madness. "Every damn lane looked the same!" The chaos in the colony was beyond his limited thinking capacity. Satish walked to a ricksha*wala* and said: "3/29" and looking at his confused look. Satish quickly realised the north-south divide. Satish somehow remembered *theen* but could in no way know what was in Hindi for "twenty nine". Finally he used all available resources, including the old lady walking by, to explain the ricksha*wala* where to take him.

Satish got a hint of the ordeal that was waiting for him.

Within two minutes the rickshaw reached its destination. Satish climbed up to the third floor. He rang the door bell. He was feeling ashamed that he had to take someone else's help for something as simple as taking a rickshaw. *Ik-kees*. He tried to remember. The door opened. A person in a pair of dirty red shorts and yellowish banian, with his face hidden inside thick beard and moustache, gave a puzzled look at Satish.

"Mohit?"

"Class."

"Class?"

"AIC."

"I see…you?"

"Nakul. Meet him there at 11:30."

"Where is AIC?"

Nakul, Mohit's roommate, told Satish how to reach AIC and quickly shut the door on him. Satish was irritated, but helpless. He came down quite upset; he did not stop to appreciate the beautiful fern kept outside a flat on the first floor.

He decided to walk down to AIC, which was near Royal Prince. The road he covered had book stalls with depressed store keepers buried behind the piles of magazines like Civil Service Times, Kurukshetra, Civil Services Chronicle and copies of the latest Rozgar Yojana; male IAS aspirants at the road corner tea shops discussing sustainable agriculture, Integrated Missile Development Programme, types of female aspirants, Y2k problem, Gandhi-Irwin Pact and the like; a magnificent white *gurudwara* with a bright, golden top; the under-construction elevated corridor of the Delhi Metro; IAS aspirant couples doing interesting, combined study near the tea shops by the coaching centres; roadside brawls over serious issues like overtaking one's car without permission; freshers seeking advice from veterans like Mohit who were losing their youth in appearing and reappearing in the exam; and IAS aspirants intensely debating the UPSC reforms needed to make the exam a more objective and a less painful one for all of them.

Satish located AIC. He still had around 30 minutes with him; he anchored at the tea shop outside AIC. Bought a stick of Classic Milds and lit it. While the *chotu* was making tea Satish happened to overhear the nearby conversation.

"...don't have money now. My...useless father asked me to stop all this preparation stuff and head back home. He wants me to find a job and get married. I managed to appear in the exam twice...but his patience has run out."

"What rubbish?!"

"Leave it yaar...that old man will not understand...he does not know what IAS is about."

Satish did not know how to react; he just collected his cup of tea from *chotu* and concentrated more on the conversation. He was very curious to know the full story. He also wanted to share his story with them; but tried hard and stayed away.

Fifteen more minutes. Satish walked across the road and climbed up the stairs to reach the AIC office on the first floor. A small photograph of Goddess Saraswati was placed on the clerk's desk. Reams and reams of study material wrapped in yellow covers were dumped to his sides. Satish interrupted the clerk who was busy with his calculator, "I want to meet Mohit..." The clerk was more interested in his calculator. After waiting for a moment Satish moved towards the notice board. *"2 selections in Top 10 in 1999 results. 27 Selections in the last 4 years"* A brochure with that caption was pinned on the notice board. Below the caption there were two large photos and 25 tiny photos. Satish remembered seeing something similar to this on back covers of some magazines like Competition Success Review.

In a few minutes the doors of the lecture hall opened and a huge crowd of students rushed out like a herd of sheep. Some were puny. Some carried long registers. Some looked fair. Some were over-weight.

A few had come in formal dresses. Some were balding. Some were from the North East. Some had huge shoulder bags that reminded Satish of his days at Prime. Some looked worried. Some were from remote villages. Many were cheerful. The whole area was noisy reminding Satish of the Madurai bus-stand. He could only hear discrete words like *interview board, IPS, dowry, DM, luck, top 50, status, T N Seshan, October 17th, Nagaland-cadre, tiffinwala, five attempts, zoology, Bipin Chandra, corruption, power* etc.

The last person to come out was a man dressed in formals and with a few slim books and a white board marker in his hand. He seemed to be explaining something to the two girls and a guy who were walking with him. After clarifying their doubts he reached the clerk's desk for the tea flask. Satish followed him.

That person in formals was about to have his first sip when he noticed Satish, and gave a questioning look.

"Satish, Madurai...Mohit..Mohit sir?"

The other man was so happy to hear that, "Satish! Yeah! I was expecting you. Sorry I had to rush here for an unplanned class in the morning. It was an orientation class for the new aspirants. Rao sir had actually planned to handle it himself...but he got tied up. You met Nakul?"

"Yes, I met that lousy specimen", that was how Satish wanted to reply. But he just said, "Yes sir."

"So, you are all set for the tough days ahead?"

Satish did not know what to tell him. He was not sure whether his father would have told Mohit about his actual intentions or his father would have done something like he had done in the Collectorate some years back. Satish was clueless; he tried to change the topic.

"I need to find a room."

"You can get settled in a day or two. No problem! There is another orientation class after a couple of days…you attend that. The GS (General Studies) classes start on October 17th. What are your optionals? You may join history or psycho (psychology) here; they are starting the same day as GS."

Satish was disappointed that he was not able to divert Mohit's mind from the IAS exams. He tried once again, "How is the food…?"

"There are many tiffin*wala*s. Right from Bengali to Gujarati to Kerala…you find all kinds of tiffin*wala*s here. Well…there is a good Tamil tiffin*wala* too. I can get his number for you. There are many aspirants from Tamil Nadu these days…you know? There are many from Maharastra and Andhra too. The Exam is getting highly competitive…people with master's degrees…even doctors…surgeons, and those with many years of industry work experience…everyone is taking the Exam these days…it's getting tougher...also too many engineers!"

Mohit's life seemed to be revolving only around IAS preparation. Satish did not know what to do. He also had the dilemma of how to reply – whether as someone showing interest in the exams or someone who was here just to pass one year before getting back to his liquor business. "The latter would be a great disrespect to my dad in front of this chatterbox Mohit." So Satish showed some interest to whatever Mohit told him about the exam and asked something from time to time. They walked out of AIC and reached the tea shop outside.

Satish asked, "Since when have you been taking classes here, sir?"

"I am from Orissa...after my graduation from Cuttack, I worked for a few years in Bhubaneshwar...saved some money and came to Delhi in 1995. I did not clear my first Prelims in 1996. I went till the interview in my next two attempts. My interview mark this year was pathetic – only 80. Had it been even 110, I would have been selected in some service. Probably in IRS...and doing my Foundation Course in Mussourie...probably trekking in the Himalayas" Mohit continued without even bothering to see whether Satish was listening to him or looking at the girls around, "...My last roommate had scored 225 in the interview...he is such a dumb fellow...one of the best fools you would come across! 2-2-5!! Can you believe that?! His score in the written papers was also not bad...I don't know how he managed that. He is an IAS officer now!", Mohit turned sad and said, "I will be thirty next year and have only one more chance left...I decided to take that final attempt in 2000 with you all…I was too shocked by the results I was not ready for the Prelims that was just four days after the results…I have only one chance left…the last bullet...golden bullet."

Satish was experiencing the heights of torture. He was reminded of his Class XII physics classes. "Perhaps they were better", he told himself. Mohit was busy with his autobiography, "…I joined AIC in its very first batch – we were only 13 aspirants that time." he continued proudly, "Look at the crowd now!! This is all due to Rao sir's sincerity and hard work…dedication and commitment. He works from six in the morning to midnight…We got two positions in the top 10 this year – rank 3 and rank 8! That is a record for any coaching institute…just four years into the field and already twenty seven selections. Twenty seven in just four years! Simply incredible!!"

Satish, who was not even aware of the total marks allotted for the interview, tried to remind Mohit what he had actually wanted to know, "Er…I mean, since when have you been taking classes here?"

"It started this May with some topics in psychology for this Mains batch. I did not want to go home this year...after my bad result. But I was getting mad sitting and preparing again. I approached Rao sir. He was kind to me," pointing in the direction of the AIC building, Mohit added, "Some students have given sir good feedback about my classes for the Mains. So, for the Prelims-cum-Mains session starting in two weeks, sir has asked me to handle some topics in GS too, probably statistics and ancient history. These classes are a good change for me, I also get some cash...how long can I trouble my parents? It has already been four years now...I want to return home – only as an IAS officer" Mohit continued. "By the way...please don't call me sir. I am one like you...only an IAS aspirant. Just one more faceless aspirant."

For a moment Satish wondered how Nakul and Mohit managed to stay in the same flat. "Probably it is only because of this chatterbox that Nakul is like that!" Satish controlled his laughter and sincerely nodded to whatever Mohit said. Satish also imagined what would have happened during Mohit's interview. "The interview board would have got bored! Poor fellows!"

Satish reached his Royal Prince room around 10 PM. He was quite full after the *rotis, paneer,* chicken and fried rice in a nearby shack. But he still missed the soft *idlis* and spicy *sambhar* of Madurai. "Is my life going to be with people like Mohit for one whole year?" Satish could not sleep well till midnight. "What am I going to do in this sea of IAS aspirants?...How about going back to Madurai tomorrow?"

Suddenly he got up, switched on the light and hurriedly opened his suitcase. Threw stuff like clothes and bed sheets and reached for something at the bottom. It was the framed, group photograph of The Desperados taken near the lake, in Kodaikanal. He cried.

Satish was disturbed by a high-pitched, rhythmic voice that was not dying down. He got up and peeped out of the hotel window to find it was someone with an empty polythene sack going around on an old bicycle shouting, *"Raddiwala"*. Daily around 9:30 in the morning the *raddiwalas* start competing among themselves for old newspapers, empty bottles, polythene covers, outdated IAS preparation material and other such items in the locality. Satish realised it was time to get started. "Just a year…somehow I have to pass the time. After all the Maharaja-IAS deal is not a bad one." After much difficulty he located Famous Fruit Juice; there were a few IAS aspirants having some grape coloured shake; Satish stared at the fairest girl; she too looked at Satish for a moment. Mohit had told him that Navin the property dealer lived bang opposite the juice stall. Satish knocked on the door and waited for some time after which a short, bubbly person in a safari suit appeared.

"Good morning sirji!"

Satish smiled and said "I need a room for rent…Mohit sent me here."

"Bilkulji! Aap south se?" asked Navin.

Satish gave a confused look and hesitatingly said, "IAS…coaching."

"Okay…we can go now…I am asking if you are from Tamil Nadu?" Navin said while laughing.

Satish smiled and nodded. He was actually irritated. Navin kickstarted his bike. Satish took the pillion seat. Both of them did not wear helmets.

In about three minutes they reached a five-storied apartment near the huge MCD (Municipal Corporation of Delhi) water tank of the area. But during those three minutes neither Navin closed his mouth nor did Satish utter a word. Navin was apparently explaining his ultimately boring life history in an exciting way, in his own peculiar blend of Hindi and English. Satish could figure out roughly that this fellow was probably from somewhere near Dehradun, did not go to college, and had something to do with Rameswaram. "Probably he had been there on a pilgrimage with his family or for his father's funeral."

By the end of the day Satish was thoroughly upset. Navin had shown him three places. The first one was a spacious, marble floored double-seater room on the second floor; there was already one aspirant, with history and physics as the optionals. The room had two huge windows. It seemed it was the person's third attempt and he had been in that same room for the last four years. Satish took a look at the room and got intimidated by what he saw – three wooden racks full of books in all colours and sizes, latest magazines, a dozen note books and reams of loose sheets with something scribbled lying scattered all over the room. A 5-foot pile of newspapers in a corner reminded Satish of the Pisa Tower. Satish also noticed a big poster with the caption *"Where there is a will; there is a way"*. There were also three other posters – Swami Vivekananda in colour, physical map India showing mountain ranges, rivers etc, and the third was the famous one of Mahatma Gandhi during the Dandi March. Satish quickly decided to look for some other room.

The second room was in a flat like that of Mohit's. Third floor. 3 BHK-flat. One of those rooms had on its door the famous low angle still of an angry, young Amir Khan from *Sarfarosh*. It had the caption *"A reason to live"*. Hardeep Singh stayed in that room. The other room had a person from Bikaner. The rooms were not even half the size of Satish's room in Madurai. The hall was a little bigger than the other rooms and stuffed with many pairs of footwear, old and torn newspapers, unused air coolers, some worn out clothes, broken chairs and a fridge in coma stage. The empty room had huge windows that opened into the balcony of the adjacent apartment hardly ten feet away from this one.

The third flat where Navin took Satish was a 2 BHK. One room was already occupied. The room was an architectural wonder in the sense that without getting out of it one could never make out whether it was day or night, sunny or rainy, festival or strike outside. The owner of the house proudly told Satish, "You can study without any worry and disturbance. The student who was here earlier is an IPS officer now...in J&K." The landlord also promised to extend his UPS connection to this room for an extra charge of Rs.150 per month.

"I cannot give you that much", Satish was shouting at Navin who had asked for a brokerage of 15 days' rent for the second flat they had seen. Building no. 4/5, third floor. The rent was Rs.1600 per month. Electricity charges extra Rs.100 per month. Extra Rs.400 for electricity during winters if room heaters were used. The landlord also demanded a month's rent as advance. "Rascals! I am yet to see such business men in my life!" Finally Satish and Navin settled for Rs.750 as brokerage. Satish was feeling helpless without being able to communicate properly. "Had it been Madurai I would have finished the deal at 400." Navin was happy that he did not understand English well.

He dropped Satish near Royal Prince and said, "*Theek hai sirji*...all the best. Any time, any help...no problem" while thrusting his business card in Satish's right hand and zoomed ahead on his bike.

Satish started to pack his stuff in the hotel room. He felt there was something strange about this whole area. All the buildings here were a mere unplanned extension of the ground floors, where the landlords invariably stayed. It looked haphazard, crowded and dingy. Luckily for him, there was a generous window in his new-found room. The window opened into the next building; a 7-foot by-lane separated the two apartments. "These buildings cannot be called apartments; these are merely houses that started growing to accommodate the countless IAS aspirants who poured in year after year." There was no question of a lift in any of these buildings. No question of a separate compound wall or an enclosure. No question of a watchman. In many cases no question even of the government approval. The buildings were bundled one after the other. In some places it would not be difficult even for obese uncles to fly from one building to the other.

Only the pigeons seemed to be happy and free in those buildings.

In the next two hours' time Satish opened the flat with the key the landlord had given him on receiving Rs.3300. He was at the door of his new home – a worn-out 10' X 8' room. It was to the immediate left when one entered the flat. Unlike the other two rooms this room had an attached bathroom. The lanky Hardeep stayed in the middle room. The third room had a tiny lock on its latch. The common bathroom was to the right. Satish entered his room gasping. He threw the suitcase and two bags he had got, switched on the fan and just fell on the cot like a log of wood. Three floors! Sixty six steps!

The fan started to speed up with a rhythm. Satish focused on the blackened blades of the fan that were visible now and then, depending on their position in the dimly lit room. He breathed deeply.

Then he turned to his right slowly to have a better view of his room. The room craved for a bare minimum coat of distemper. There was an *India Today* 1999 calendar pasted on the wall to his right, just above the dusty desk. He turned his head. There was a dark wooden cupboard just in front of his stretched legs. A long, sticker with the image of Lord Krishna blessing Arjun, who was on his knees with his bow and quiver beside him, was pasted on the left door. *"Do your duty; do not have expectations"*. That caption irritated Satish, who was in no mood for any kind of advice. "Why is everyone here fond of posters with quotes?" He quickly turned left. On the wall adjoining his cot there was a dirty bulb-holder; it had waited for ages for a bulb; it was still waiting.

Satish closed his eyes. He tried hard to stop his tears. He almost succeeded.

After a while was about to change his pair of jeans when someone knocked on his door. Satish pulled up the zipper and opened the door.

"I'm Hardeep."

"Hello...Satish."

"First-timer? What are your optionals?"

That was one of the most irritating questions for Satish. But it was the most natural opener for anyone in that area. Satish tried to look calm and said, "Not yet decided…" in a little confused tone.

"Mine are mech and psycho. I did mech in Kharagpur. This is my second attempt." Hardeep continued with a pride, "IPS first choice. Yours? IAS?" Satish was more annoyed and confused. He was not even aware that such a complexly-mixed feeling had been there in him, before he reached this den of civil service aspirants. He cursed his father sitting at Maharaja before replying, "Kha..rug..pur?? Where is it? I'm from Madurai EC Engineering College. BE computer science."

Hardeep just smiled and said, "Oh…CompSci! Why civil services?" Hardeep was just too curious to know the dreams of his new flat-mate. "Hardeep…My stomach is eating me…need to go down for food." Hardeep laughed and rushed to his room.

He returned with a banana, "Take this before you go…see you… Sorry, forgot your name…"

"Satish. Thanks. See you later." Satish did not change his pair of jeans; he got out right away and locked his room with the lock he had used for chaining his suitcase during the train journey.

Before rushing out of the flat he quickly moved towards Hardeep's room and knocked the door softly. Hardeep opened the door, he was having food. Pointing to the dustbin kept in the corner near the bathroom, Satish curiously asked "Do you drink?" Hardeep nodded. Satish was very happy. Though Satish had seen a huge crowd outside the liquor shops he had not even imagined that the studious civil service aspirants would drink. "The crowd is of useless people like me; IAS aspirants would not be wasting time here." But he had noticed that empty Haywards bottle near the dustbin when Navin had shown him the flat. That empty beer bottle near the dustbin had given Satish a ray of hope – "This area is probably not as boring as I thought." Satish was excited. He hugged Hardeep quickly before rushing down for food.

He decided to try something new menu and crossed Shankar road to reach New Rajinder Nagar. Mohit had told him about Ulan Bator, the no-frills Chinese restaurant. On the other side of the road near the tri-junction, Satish came across a loud bunch of college students. A few were smoking, some were sitting on their bikes, and one was engrossed in whistling. All of them were rather noisy. Satish remembered *The Desperados.* "Why did my father give me such a punishment – firstly by separating me from my friends, and then by dropping me in this jungle of IAS Exam?" He felt like a refugee.

He continued to walk towards the Chinese eat-out. But he stopped at the STD-ISD PCO on the way. He got inside that transparent cabin with a yellow frame and dialed Madurai. He wanted to tell his father how badly he missed all of them. He wanted to blast his father for pushing him into this dungeon called IAS Exams. "How did it matter whether I knew about the medieval art, three-stage nuclear cycle etc or not; I want to sell liquor anyway." He wanted to cry about his clueless and isolated life in this prison full of strange people and subjects.

There were three rings. Rajaraman picked the phone. By the time the mutual hellos got over the conversation progressed like that of a daily status report (DSR) – about meeting Mohit, Delhi weather, getting settled in a new room etc. Satish was craving to vent his frustration and anger, but postponed it after every sentence. Rajaraman was very happy; he could already feel a sense of responsibility in his son's voice. "It was not a bad decision to send my boy to Delhi. He will be a winner!" Satish got restless like a trapped mouse. He kept waiting for the right chance to open his heart and shout it out. Satish's heart was beating louder to explode, it was then he noticed a familiar face at the shop to which the phone booth was attached.

The person looked somewhat like Mohit. "Yes…it is him! But who is that cute one near him? How did this boring fellow manage this black beauty?! May be she is one of his students…yes, she is carrying some books. But in this damn place everyone carries some book or the other! Looks like these two are quite close… friends. I hope this fellow is not boring her with his interview marks…." "Is it possible?" Rajaraman's voice jumped loudly out of the telephone receiver and abruptly stopped Satish's thesis on Mohit and the girl next to him. Satish realised that his father was on the line; without even having the slightest idea of what his father had been saying, he just said "Where there is a will, there is a way daddy...classes start on October 17th. Good night."

Satish waited inside the cabin for those two to leave the shop before he came out to pay for his call. Then he proceeded in the opposite direction, towards Ulan Bator. He reached it in 50 long steps. It was a small, open-air eat-out on the roadside. It was crowded. Satish went through the 4-foot price list banner. Only a few items like tomato soup, noodles and Manchurian sounded familiar to him. He went through the menu – *American chopsey. Chicken spring roll.* But who was that one with Mohit? *Singapore noodles. Szechuan chicken.* How did that idiot manage this? *Chicken Manchurian.* Probably they are just friends. But what if? *Chicken-paneer soup. Mongolian lamb.*

Mohit and the girl were walking slowly in the opposite direction. They appeared dark, yellowish orange in colour. A sodium vapour lamp was exactly above their heads.

As they walked further, the light dimmed; their shoulders brushed against each other.

Satish was happy the next morning when he saw something like a food packet hanging from the latch of the door to his flat. He was happier when he felt and concluded it had *idlis* and coconut *chutney*. There was also a chit written in Tamil. *Morning – Rs.11, Lunch (meals): Rs.21, Dinner – Rs.11. Advance – Rs.300. Senthil. Ph-2532081.* Navin must have arranged this, Satish guessed. But his happiness was short-lived when he opened and tasted the *idlis*. They were not the kind of *idlis* he had known for the past twenty years or so, this item was something totally new and tasteless – but had an incredibly close resemblance to the *idli* he was familiar with. Satish felt like throwing those *idlis* at Navin and Senthil but somehow managed to eat all four. *Chutney* was okay.

Clueless about what to do next, Satish went to Hardeep's room. There was no reply even after two knocks on the door. The third room was still locked. Satish got back to his room. He was utterly bored and started cursing his father again. He smoked for two hours. "What will Kumar be doing this moment? Good old days of The Desperados. Why is my dad crazy? Maharaja: 2005. How to pass one year like this? This bad food. These boring fellows. Should I go back to Madurai now? Who was the girl with that chatterbox?"

Satish dressed quickly and walked down the three floors to climb a different three. "What do you mean? You are bored?!" Mohit asked while gesturing Satish to get into his room. That was the first time Satish had actually entered a civil service aspirant's room for a time-pass conversation. Earlier he had only glanced at three such rooms during his room-hunt with Navin.

Mohit's room was neat. Not even a single sheet of paper was out of its place. It was like a Japanese factory – everything had a place and everything was at its place. The books were perfectly arranged in three steel racks. Satish found this room equally intimidating. Mohit asked him to be seated. There was a thin book, some loose sheets of paper and a capless pen lying on the desk. The ceiling fan was motionless.

Mohit asked, "So how's life here? You met Navin?" while closing the pen. "My life is not as interesting as yours", that's what Satish wanted to comment but he just said, "Yes, thank you…I moved to a new room. 4/5. It is fine. But I am tired moving of up and down the three floors!"

"Oh…you got that? That is a good one. I had been there long back. But which room…there are three rooms, right?...I had a friend there long back. He is in the railways now…posted as Area Manager… somewhere in Hubli", Mohit went on.

"The one to the left when you enter the flat" Satish barged in.

Satish noticed a physical map of India pasted on the wall. There were two other equally large political maps – one of India and one of the world. Satish stood up and moved towards the racks. Out of sheer boredom he had a close look at the books. First rack. There were four huge books at the bottom – India Year Book – for the years 1996, 1997, 1998 and 1999. Satish was too lazy to lift the books and open the pages. There was a Manorama Year Book series besides that pile. He moved directly to the top shelf where he noticed books like Spectrum Modern Indian History, some school text books, a guide book for The Constitution of India, Orient Longman School Atlas, Unique Quintessence for GS, etc. Mohit said, "Just a minute" and moved out of the room. Satish continued with some more time-pass. He moved to the second rack. This had a few books on psychology. Robert A. Baron was the top most one. There were reams of photocopied material in the middle shelves of this rack. *The Indian psyche* was also amidst the handouts. The shelf at the bottom was empty.

"Have you decided your optionals?" Mohit entered with a water bottle.

"Psychology" Satish told him bluntly and continued looking around.

"That is good. I too have taken that as my first optional. It is a scoring paper…but I could manage only 305 marks this time. In fact, Rao sir is well-known for psychology. During his first….."

Satish did not know where and how Mohit's talk show ended. Satish moved towards the opposite wall where a 3' X 4' white sheet of thermacol was mounted. He walked close to it to find a few bits of paper with some scribbling, key points of personality theories and a few newspaper cuttings with some statistics like India's GDP, IX Five-Year Plan targets etc, pinned to it. In one of those sheets Mohit had also made an schedule for study. In another corner of the thermacol board Satish noticed: *Mohit – Do or Die. FINAL attempt.* He bent and reached the third, rack kept below this thermacol sheet. Satish felt the whole room was exclusively arranged with the single goal of terrifying him. There was a bulky Concise Oxford dictionary, three books that contained the previous year's question papers, The Hindu Survey of Agriculture and Glimpses of World History. Mohit finished his talk somewhere and got back to his desk to put those loose sheets of papers in order. He raised his voice and said, "Do not get scared…many of these books are not needed for the exam. I just have them."

That was when Satish spotted a familiar face on the cover of a book. It was Dr.A.P.J.Abdul Kalam. *Wings of Fire*. So far Satish had not opened even a single book kept there. But somehow he felt like opening that book; and that proved to be interesting for him. A handwritten line on the first page of the book. "To my dearest Mohit…Wish you the very best in your life. Forever with love, Selvi." Satish closed the book with "Yes, I know" and a dirty smile that Mohit, who was still busy with those loose sheets of paper, did not notice. Mohit without turning his face started, "You see Satish, IAS preparation is…" Satish did not bother to listen beyond that.

One full week had passed since Satish had reached Delhi. Beyond the first two days when he was busy with the room hunt and then shopping for some basic items like a soap box, bucket, mosquito mat etc Satish had not done anything; he did not know what to do. It was 6 in the evening and Satish was sitting in his room having done nothing since the evening tea he had an hour back. He was smoking. He had spent the day with his usual routine of food, cigarettes and sleep. *Seven days of hell.* He was feeling like a sinking ship – his crazy father, thrice-a-day cruelty in the name of *idli* and meals, helpful but boring Mohit, loneliness in the room without even a single soul to talk to, language barrier, solitary beer sessions, nice but sincere Hardeep, and many more like the intimidating books that came in many colours and sizes – all these were pushing him down every moment. Satish did not want to associate with anything even remotely associated with the Exam preparation. Usually he did not even listen to Mohit beyond his first three sentences as it invariably related to the IAS exams, optionals, interview, Prelims, coaching etc. And strangely for him, Satish did not have anyone to talk with on any topic other than the Exam preparation. In fact he did not know anyone other than Mohit and Hardeep.

He wished to be a friend of the person in the room across the lane; the room was hardly ten feet away from his room's huge windows. "When does she come out? I see the clothes on the balcony change daily." But the balcony door of the room never seemed to open. He had impatiently waited many times for a chance to peep into that room; but to no good. Left with no choice he had wandered alone in the streets of Old Rajinder Nagar without any purpose other than having a cup of tea and smoking. "What kind of life is this?" The third person in his flat too seemed to be busy running after some classes, books purchase and relatives, and his door was rarely seen unlocked. Satish had drunk alone the previous two nights. He did not want to disturb Hardeep, who seemed to be immersed in his books 24 X 7. It seemed impossible for Satish to pass the next year like this. "The Maharaja-IAS deal looked simple but was like cancer." He had come with some plans of having a great time in Delhi before taking charge of his business, but if things went like this he would definitely be mad by that time. "When will I be out of this torture cell?"

Only over the phone he really got to talk properly. But then again he never found the right chance to shout at his father. He had planned it thrice in the last four days but never managed to go beyond the DSR. Satish finally talked to Kumar the previous night after trying a number of times in the previous week. But the former was shocked to know that one of their trucks had met with a serious accident at a railway crossing a few days back and things were in pretty bad shape at Kumar's end.

"Don't worry…business will have its ups and downs. Things will be okay soon…you be cool", he had consoled Kumar the previous night.

Satish made a quick decision. He threw the unfinished Milds in the wash basin outside the room, dressed up and rushed towards Royal Prince. The manager there recognised him. Satish called for Vijay, the room attendant. They two of them came out of the hotel and stood by the tea shop next to it. Without wasting any more time Satish quickly asked Vijay something. He scratched his head and nodded. They went to the nearest PCO. Vijay called up someone and spoke for less than a minute and hung up.

Satish thrust a Rs.500-note into Vijay's hands. "Thank you *saab!*" said Vijay before getting back into Royal Prince.

Satish roamed the streets of Old Rajinder Nagar for almost two hours, till 8:45 PM. He had smoked four cigarettes; had had a glass of lemon soda; even aimlessly browsed the book store. He wanted to talk to someone, but did not want to call his father. He did not want to go back to, room either. He could think of only Mohit. Left with no choice Satish climbed the three floors to reach Mohit's flat.

Nakul opened the door. He looked irritated as usual. After opening the door, and a short *Hi*, he got back into his room to resume his studies. Satish walked to Mohit's room and knocked on the door timidly. The door opened.

"Oh…Satish?! What is the matter? How are you?"

"I'm fine. Just came...."

"Well...sit..." Mohit continued diffidently, "...You look upset."

"Is it? Nothing like that..." replied Satish, trying to remain calm.

"Come on man... just tell me. What's it?"

"Am perfect....just came for the book list. What are the books I need to buy?" That was the only way Satish could have managed Mohit. And that worked. Mohit lost himself in the world of books that one needed for the Prelims 2000. He thoroughly explained to Satish the pros and cons of various authors, for every subject in the GS paper. "Bipin Chandra is a must for modern Indian history." He even got up once to pick up a book from one of the two big racks and showed something to Satish. Satish looked at the book and nodded. "You said your first optional was psychology, right?" Satish nodded without hearing a single word.

Mohit started with the book-list for the psychology optional for Prelims. He also picked the tiny book with the previous years' question papers to show something interesting to Satish. "Can you believe this?" Then he progressed with his lecture on various books available in the market. Both of them were deeply engrossed – in their different worlds. "We have to keep the books to the minimum possible number...get the basics right – that is enough".

Once the lecture was over Mohit took two A4 sheets and starting writing out the booklist; he also included some selected tips from what he had explained till then. Satish was through with his thoughts and now tried to focus on what Mohit was up to. He noticed Mohit sincerely writing out the book list for him. He felt bad. Mohit handed him the booklist. "Here we go...but tell me before you buy any of them. I know some bookstores which give you more than 30-35% discount." Mohit stretched his arms and said, "Okay...it is almost 10 now. You can also have some food here. I have lots of work to do tonight. Rao sir had asked me to meet him tomorrow."

After about 20 minutes Satish came walking down the stairs with the neatly folded booklist in his hand. His heartbeat was getting louder. His face remained calm. He reached the main road. For a moment Satish thought he should meet Vijay and walked towards Royal Prince. But he quickly turned back and started moving to his room.

On the way he stopped at a liquor shop and a medical shop for less than a minute.

Five minutes past midnight there was a slight knock on Satish's door.

Just before the dawn broke we could see a middle aged lady move out of Satish's room. Someone was waiting for her downstairs in a two wheeler.

PART III: NOOSE TIGHTENS

"Good morning! This class is to give you a clear picture about the Exam as a whole. We will touch upon important areas like choosing the optional papers, time management and effective planning. You may interrupt me during the lecture…in case you need some clarifications. But before that I would like to remind all of you of the hare and tortoise story that we have heard many times..." Sitting in the last row of the free, open-for-all orientation class Satish became a bit interested on hearing about the hare and tortoise. He looked at Rao, the owner-director of Achieve IAS Coaching. Mohit was standing next to Rao. "Clearing this Exam is like that race. Though many of you have an impressive academic record, I would like to stress – only discipline and hard work can make you realise your dream. Nothing else matters. Do not be complacent. Follow the class notes regularly. Try to get a rank in the first attempt itself. It is possible even to top the Exam in the very first attempt. Some have done it!" Rao continued, "On a lighter note... I hope by now you would have heard this... it is said people come to Old Rajinder Nagar for IAS preparation when they are *bhaiyas* and *didis*...and by the time they leave this place they are uncles and aunties!" Everyone giggled. But Rao continued rather seriously, "I feel really bad when I see many of my old students still preparing...even many sincere students have failed to clear the Exam..."

He raised his voice and said, "For those who feel your academics has never been good – just remember ultimately it was not the gifted hare that won the race but it was the disciplined tortoise. And above all remember there is Someone above us and He always gives us the best, whether we like it or not!" Rao said pointing to the off-white false ceiling. For the next one hour Rao animatedly explained the whole story on cracking the IAS Exam. Most of the aspirants took down notes in their long registers or loose sheets of papers. Satish had not even opened his pen. He did not bother to carry a register. Prof.S.S.R.Venkata Rao had started AIC after quitting his profession at Hindu College, Delhi. Both his daughters were IFS officers; one of them was serving in Iran and the other one in Mexico.

Satish was not able to concentrate, naturally. His mind kept jumping. He missed many important points; but somehow got to hear a few details like "...the Mains Exam is for 2000 marks and the interview is for 300 marks...." Whenever he got bored with peeping out of the window or surveying at the crowd or playing with his pen, he tried to listen to the lecture. Occasionally whenever his eyes closed, a thousand kingfishers happily danced for a moment.

Priety Zinta. The fairest lady Satish had seen till that day, a year back in Mani Ratnam's *Dil Se*. Other than her, nowhere in his circle in Madurai had he come across strikingly fair girls. Now he was so excited that there was a never-seen-before-type girl to his left, just two rows ahead. She was wearing bright red ear-studs and a white top. She was religiously taking down every word Rao uttered. "Sir, what rank should I get to become IPS?" someone from the first rows asked. Rao thought for a moment before answering that. Mohit smiled. Satish was too busy – with the ear-studs and the curled hair strands dangling near them.

After a while Satish was able to hear a familiar voice. He turned away from the split AC, at which he had been staring for the last few minutes, and realised that Mohit had started his part of the lecture. Rao was seated; he was sipping from the glass of water. One could hear a pin drop in the class. "Oh! No! He is talking about the book list! This is going to go on for another half an hour!" Satish turned towards the AC again. He was just checking out the key details printed on it like the brand name, capacity, instructions for usage, warranty period etc. There were a few questions to Mohit from the aspirants. He answered them in his typical style of J to A to Z – not just A to Z. "It is going to be a real fight for one full year…but this victory will make you and your parents proud for the rest of your life." Rao resumed his speech, pointing to the crowd; his eyes were wide open. A few nodded in agreement. Many others did not nod, but agreed. But the whole atmosphere was charged up as if a General was pumping up his fighters in a war field. Mohit was looking serious. Satish was a bit disappointed. He could not locate that dark beauty in the crowd. "Is she not a student here? But I'm sure her name is Selvi."

It was the last few minutes of the orientation class. Most of the students looked determined to take the Exams even the next day. Rao looked satisfied. He could see the commitment and quest for success in most of the eyes. He felt happy that he was doing his part in eradicating poverty, in reducing crime, in creating effective diplomats and other officers who formed the steel frame of the country; he was satisfied with his role in shaping the future of India. After a while it seemed Rao asked something and the whole class thunderously shouted, "Yes sir! I promise!"

Satish was unfazed; he was looking out of the window through the partly closed Venetian blind. He was missing Madurai.

The person next to Satish tapped Satish's hand, but Satish was lost in the tea shop down the road; he tapped once again and then held Satish's arm and gave it a light shake. Satish jerked and landed inside the class. "Yes...you gentleman in the last row. Do you have any question?" Rao was pointing at Satish. A chill ran down Satish's spine when he quickly realised the whole class had been watching him, waiting for him to turn away from the window and answer Rao. There were a few giggles and murmurs.

The fair girl with the red studs also curiously turned to see who it was. Mohit too, disappointedly looked at Satish. Satish gripped his pen tightly and in a moment, cleared his throat to ask, "Sir, why should I write this Exam?"

"How are things now?"

"Okay buddy...we have settled everyone, including the insurance fellows, police, local press...quite relieved! Am very sorry *da*...was tight. Tell me your story..."

"That's good. Hmmm... things are okay here, now. But I can't tell you how depressing it is going to be...for one full year! We had an orientation class yesterday..."

Kumar shouted in disbelief, "What?!! You attended an IAS class?!

You have changed, my dear friend…" He mischievously added, "…you have forgotten those royal, college days!"

"Shut up you idiot! You cannot even imagine the hell I'm living in…you have to be here to believe how miserable life can get. I never thought I would land up in such a prison… we were actually living a king's life those days…the luxuries we had there.."

"I happened to meet uncle yesterday evening, near the market. He was very happy that you are preparing for the Exams…"

"Oh?! This is all due to that old man! Maharaja owner's crazy idea…I should ask him to be here for at least one week, then he would realise IAS Exam is not a joke. And IAS is not something for his stupid son!"

"My dear Desperado….don't get hyper. Just pass the time. One year is nothing! Have fun! I'm facing the grind here daily…running a business is more hellish! We are craving for holidays…a short break. You know…the last time all of us here met was – only during your farewell party. No one has time…"

"Oh…?!"

Kumar asked eagerly, "Did you see the Taj Mahal?... And what about the girls?"

"Fool… Agra is not in Delhi."

"Okay, okay….girls?"

"Yeah!! You won't believe...such fair girls! I'm clean bowled!! You come here soon...at least for these beauties from all over the country. I owe my existence here to them!"

"Really?! You got to talk with anyone?"

"Class starts tomorrow."

October 17th, 1999. There were 120 civil service aspirants in that room – roughly 700 square feet in area with walls having a huge white board, an antique-looking clock, five split ACs, two motivational posters and a compact, old fire extinguisher. Everyone seemed to show full attention to what was happening to Pakistan. Rao had started the GS sessions with the Indo-Pak relations. Usually the six-month GS sessions started with classes on Indian polity and continued with other topics like science and technology, Indian history – ancient, medieval and modern, geography, economy, biology etc before ending with foreign relations. But the coup led by General Musharraf in Pakistan made Rao take up the foreign relations classes on priority. Veterans like Mohit, Nakul, Hardeep and others, who had taken coaching and appeared in the Exams earlier sat in their rooms and prepared. First-timers usually were busy the whole day – they had two coaching classes to attend – one for GS and one for the first optional. But where was Satish? He was not in his room.

Was he at the tea shop? One could not locate him on the last bench of the class too. What a surprise…! The middle one in the first row in Rao's class looked like Satish. Yes! No doubt, it was Satish!

It was Rao's peculiar way of punishing irresponsible and arrogant students like Satish. Satish also did not want to damage Mohit's reputation further in front of Mohit's mentor Rao, so he had to comply with Rao's rules. Mohit had struggled hard to pacify Rao after Satish's stupid behaviour during the orientation class. Rao was magnanimous enough. Being the first class Satish also was too curious to miss it. Also over the last two weeks Satish had concluded that unless he visited the classes he would go mad – sitting alone smoking and drinking. Satish also could feel every one of the forty Rs.500 currency notes he had deposited at the AIC office the previous day, flying in the class. Rs.12,000 for the GS classes. Rs.8,000 for psychology. I need to be here at least for the kind of money I have paid to this old man who has studied psychology, but teaches many things including biotechnology. He also remembered the bill for the books and cursed Mohit for dumping his room with text books and magazines. It was Rs.4300, after an average discount of 25%. "I could have realised my Maharaja 2005 vision with this money!"

Quite exhausted and bored Satish reached his room after the morning GS classes for lunch. His body was crying for attention. He had not sat at one place for three hours listening to serious lectures in the last many years. In fact, in his whole life he had never attended any lecture that went on for three hours. Even in cinema halls the Intermission ensured that he had never sat at a stretch at one place beyond 90 minutes or so. Further, he had not even opened his mouth during the whole lecture; he had not played with his pen; he did not have the chance to survey the crowd. He had exciting plans of starting a conversation with one of those fair girls, but the front row seat demolished his dream. As if all this were not enough, the old man Rao maintained eye contact with him many times during the lectures. Initially Satish did not mind that but felt very uneasy and tried avoiding Rao by the end of the lecture. The experience in the first class was nothing short of a concentration camp for him.

Satish hurriedly stuffed his mouth with that amazingly tasteless items delivered as lunch. But he loved the pickle that came with the lunch packet. Also the *rasam*. While a few tiffin*walas* delivered the food in stainless steel tiffin boxes kept inside hot packs, a few bundled the menu in transparent polythene packs and hung it from the door latch of the customers. Satish's supplier was one of those. He had polythene covers of varying sizes and used them for rice, *sambhar*, *papad*, curry etc. All these small bundles were dumped into a big polythene cover; the big cover was hung from the door of Satish's room well before 1 PM. After that tasteless but heavy meal following a session at the torture cell – Satish felt like being born again! He lit a cigarette and moved towards the window.

The balcony door on the other side seemed to open. Satish got excited.

"For you…" Hardeep entered the room with a brown envelope from Madurai. He had signed and received it from the Professional Courier delivery man. Satish was unwilling to turn back that moment; still looked at Hardeep, thanked him and offered a puff while asking quite amused, "How are you able to sit and study the whole day?!" "No pains; no gains…the schedule is a bit tight today," Hardeep crisply answered, took two puffs and went back to his room. "Why is everybody philosophical here?" He quickly got back to the window. But the door was shut. It had not opened. Or did it open and was shut again? Satish, with his eyes fixed on the opposite balcony, grudgingly opened that courier from his father. There were two packets of holy ash and sindoor, the *prasadam* of the Madurai Meenakshi temple. A two-line note was attached with it. "Dear Satish, God bless you. Hope you remember what I told you at the Madras railway station. I'm sure you will make me proud. Love, Father".

PART IV: TROPICAL CYCLONE

It was the beginning of another endless day. For no reason Satish was up at 9 AM, much earlier than usual. It was also the first class of Mohit's lecture for this new batch. He had planned to start with the story of civilisation along the Indus Valley. Classes were from 10 o' clock to 1 PM. Satish was curious to see his friend teach; though he was sure it will turn out to be a boring one. Satish left his room early and tried to pass some more time at the tea shop before getting in for the lecture. As usual *chhotu* was busy making tea. Satish always wondered how this little fellow in torn clothes landed in front of this hot gas stove ever surrounded by numerous IAS aspirants like honey bees. With the very limited communication link between them Satish had figured out that little kid was called

Tinku, and he was from somewhere near Patna. Tinku understood that Satish was a *Madrasi*. Tinku's boss was a middle aged fellow, who often came for supervision and collection. Tinku lived in the verandah of his boss's house. Roger, the German Sheperd, did not mind sharing the verandah with Tinku. Once a year during Diwali, the eleven year old Tinku went home with Rs.2000 in cash to meet his parents and many siblings. Satish had an extra cup of special *chai* before entering the class.

Satish took his seat allotted in the first row. The person next to him gave a dirty look. Unlike schools and colleges most of the students here fought for the first rows in the classroom. Some hyper-active ones reached the class even an hour early – just to get a seat in the first row. Some groups of students also reserved seats on a turn basis. One of them would come early to reserve seats for others in the front rows, using anything from uncovered registers to dirty kerchiefs. But all of them unanimously envied Satish – he alone had the luxury of a permanently reserved seat, in the very first row. Some even wished they too had asked some silly questions during the orientation class. But Satish felt annoyed and ashamed at the way he was being treated – as a criminal under probation. But that was the only way to cool down Mohit and prevent the actual reports on his Delhi life from reaching his father; and that was also the only way by which Mohit was able to cool down Rao. Satish badly wished he had kept quiet during the last minute of orientation class.

It was the first time Satish would be sitting for Mohit's lecture. Though Satish rated Mohit as a boring person, he was interested in seeing how Mohit managed the class. The class became quiet. Mohit had taken his position near the white board. Satish got ready for the lecture. "I hope he does not bore us to death. Mohit-Ancient history, bad combination." The lecture started off well. But Mohit fluffed at times during the 3-hour session. The students did not bother much given the fact that it was for the first time he was teaching the subject. But Satish could feel something was wrong with his boring friend Mohit. "Did he have a fight with Selvi?" Satish found himself surrounded by thousands of high-end weapons and advanced gadgets. Mohit was tied to a steel chair under water. Oracle ordered Satish to take the smallest weapon in the third row and rush to Zacardi on the right bank of the Indus river. "That will save Mohit. That will redeem India!" Oracle said and vanished. Suddenly there was a continuous, sharp beep sound in the background. Satish found his computer screen flashing "Wake up Neo." Satish opened his eyes to see Mohit lecture on Indus valley.

Satish had watched *The Matrix* many times since the day he reached Delhi. Satish went alone for all the shows, unlike during his Madurai days.

Satish had gone for some Hindi films too – without knowing the head or tail of the language – just for the sake of killing time. But he felt that his Hindi improved with every film he watched. He wanted to see *KKHH* again.

"...were excavated in Lothal and Harappa. Okay...we end the class here." Mohit finished his lecture. Satish gave a sigh of relief.

Without waiting for any of the students to come near him with the usual set of post-lecture doubts, he waved his hand and rushed out of the class as if something was on fire. Satish had waited for the class to get over to start the talk with the girl on the next seat but was now more curious about Mohit and followed him. Mohit did not walk down the steps; he jumped; he flew. Satish tried to cope with his speed but the herd of students moving out slowed him down. Pushing a few here and there Satish too managed to reach the end of the stairs, in moments. Ricksha*walas*, fruit vendors, Maruti 800s, auto rickshaws, dozens of people. But Mohit was nowhere to be seen. Satish was disappointed to leave the story unfinished. "I know who is waiting for him." He told himself.

Satish opened the packet of *sambhar* and poured it over the mountain of white rice. But his mind was teeming with unanswered, vital questions. "What was the matter? Why did that fellow fly? Were they going to get married?" And a thousand similar ones. "Is it in any way connected with his first class?" He smashed the *papad* into many tiny pieces. "Or her birthday today and he had not met her yet?" He dumped the empty polythene covers in the dustbin outside their flat. Got back to the room and flipped the pages of the newspaper aimlessly, as if he had expected to see a news item on Mohit's flight after his first class. He put the newspaper aside and stared at the ceiling fan that was at its fastest and loudest. "I should have run faster. But those buggers did not let me go fast. Now how can I get to know the story? Or should I go to his room?"

Now it was time for Hardeep to drop in at Satish's room. According to a permanent deal they had struck they met everyday for a while in the afternoon, before Hardeep started with his post-lunch session of studies; and Satish caught up with his nap before the evening tea session and psychology classes that followed. During such daily meetings Satish usually gossiped about Mohit and his enigmatic love life, talked about the dark beauty, learnt the Hindi version for "What is your name? You are beautiful. I miss you. I'm very hungry. Get lost bastard" etc, cursed his father, sought Hardeep's tips on talking to fair and lovely girls, cribbed about the poor food, his infrequent and lonely drinking sessions, the strict Rao, the pitiable Tinku and the stingy landlord. Hardeep usually talked about his engineering days, his IPS dream, Indira Gandhi, *bhangra*, his GPA of five-point something and his batch mates who bagged top ranks in the civil service exams or were famous entrepreneurs and authors. Being a talented singer, he occasionally hummed a number or two for Satish.

They were usually Bengali songs. Satish enjoyed them, and envied Hardeep. Sometimes Hardeep permitted *listener's choice* – to which Satish invariably opted for *Nahin Saamne* from *Taal*. Hardeep was in Satish's room door as expected. Satish had a fully-loaded topic for the day – the mysterious Mohit. "My intelligent flat-mate will decode this Mohit puzzle." Satish badly wanted Hardeep's expert analysis of the situation. Hardeep took a few, slow-motion steps. He maintained a stiff upper lip. He did not utter a word. Satish was confused; he already had a problem at hand.

Hardeep slowly stretched out his hand and opened his palm. There was a neatly folded paper chit. "What?" Satish asked while picking it. Hardeep was expressionless. He turned his head towards the sticker on the cupboard, away from Satish. "Was it from Mohit?" Satish opened it anxiously. The very next moment Satish jumped in joy, hugged and kissed Hardeep, while yelling, "You Harry bastard!" Hardeep smiled and got back to his room without opening his mouth. But we could hear his hearty laughter from behind the closed door of his room. Satish was still jumping; now kissing the chit: "You are cordially invited for a "*special*" meeting with the "*director*". Mr.Hardeep Singh's room. 9 tonight. Don't miss it!!! Though Satish was not fond of Director's Special, he did not mind anything as long as he had a company to drink with.

Satish could not sleep that afternoon; he was excited. After a long gap, today, he was going to drink with someone – not just alone. He was also amused by the way Hardeep had asked him to join him for a drink. "Smart bugger!" Satish planned of accessories that he could arrange for that night. "I wish Kumar were here! I wish all the Desperados were here!" Satish's joy knew no bounds. "Should I ask Hardeep if anything is to be arranged from Royal Prince? Hey wait…but what happened to Mohit?"

Around 3:30 PM, Satish rushed out of his room, just the way Mohit did that morning. There was a register in his hand. On the pretext of getting some doubts cleared he wanted to get Mohit started. There was no other way he could disturb Mohit in the afternoon. There was no way Satish could wait till the next day to know the full story from Mohit. Satish reached the lane of 3/29. But he did not know how to enter Mohit's apartment. He waited for some time around two metres away from the building. *"Shoo…shoo"*, he made some noises while waving the register at the 4-member family of well-fed rhesus monkeys. The family had besieged Mohit's lane. The smallest one – a mischievous boy, was pulling his father's tail. The father occasionally got up to scare the little fellow away. The mother monkey was munching something peacefully. *"Gghooo gghooo"*, Satish tried different noises and matching actions. He slowly moved closer to them. The monkey family did not care about Satish. He held his register tightly while inching ahead. Only one metre away.

All of a sudden the little one quickly turned and jumped towards Satish. Satish was shell-shocked. He dropped the register and ran for his life before halting at the street corner, some 50 metres away from the monkeys. The little monkey had a good laugh about it. Satish looked around and felt happy that no one noticed his act of bravery.

About 15 minutes later, the family moved away voluntarily.

Satish did not wait even to breathe. He just ran up the stairs of Mohit's apartment; reached the door and took two seconds to take deep breaths before pressing the door bell. "Oh…that boring young man Nakul would come now..." Satish took a few more deep breaths. His heart beat slowed down. His head was feeling cooler. But no one seemed to open the door.

"Is there any connection between the Indus valley inscriptions and the painted grey ware of southern Tamil Nadu?" Satish revised the question that he was supposed to ask Mohit. Satish did not exactly understand the meaning of the question; but Hardeep did.

Satish got restless and raised his hand to press the bell again. The door opened with a click sound and a sharp movement. Satish could not believe his eyes and he shouted in excitement, "Selvi?!!!", before shutting his mouth quickly. It was the girl whom he had seen with Mohit in the PCO some days back. She looked disturbed; darker in complexion than Satish had remembered her; and now surprised.

Satish instantaneously realised his blunder – he was not supposed to have uttered that name. He was not supposed to have seen her before. He was not supposed to have given a connection between the PCO-girl and Wings of Fire. "What a blunder! Why am I being such a fool? Anyway…this has got to be Selvi definitely…I hope she does not form a bad impression of me." The girl gave him a dirty look.

"Mohit? My name is Satish"

She did not speak; but her expression said a lot, including – "So…you are that one who is in Delhi for time pass." She nodded and gestured Satish to get in. Satish felt uneasy. "Actually it would have been better if that Nakul fellow had been here, instead of this dark beauty…hopeless boys are any day better than angry girls." He followed her to Mohit's room. "What is this girl doing here? She looks pretty even when being upset!! Lucky Mohit!" The girl pushed open the partly-closed door of Mohit's room. Very unlike his room, things including a few books were scattered all over the room. It did not look like a Japanese factory anymore. In the middle of the room, there was a suitcase wide open. Mohit was not at his study desk. Satish looked around. In the corner of the room, Satish could see Mohit with his face buried in his palms. Satish did not know what it was about and how to react. He could not guess anything. He turned and looked the girl, expecting something. She was silent.

Mohit got up and walked towards these two and sat on the cot. The girl resumed her work. She put some more essentials into the open suitcase. She carefully placed some cash at the bottom of the suitcase. Satish could not make out what was going on. "Are they eloping or something?" He looked at Mohit. Satish could just figure out something grossly bad had happened somewhere and probably Mohit was planning to set things right. "Have they got married without telling their parents? Hmmm…love is blind...totally blind." Mohit was in a state of extreme shock to even see Satish. He looked as if he was in the midst of an endless, directionless ocean. Satish hesitatingly got up and switched on the fan. The girl went out of the room. Satish found it odd to keep quiet, and followed her. He did not want to talk to Mohit. The girl entered the washroom; came back with a set of items like toothpaste etc. Satish stopped her before she entered Mohit's room with: "What is the matter? Can't you open your mouth?" That was when someone opened the door of the flat and entered. It was Nakul. He walked straight towards them. He was carrying a big polythene cover with some stuff. He gave it to the girl. He also took some cash out of his pocket and handed it over. All the three entered Mohit's room. Satish was finding it difficult to control his restlessness. The suitcase was closed and made to stand upright. The shoulder bag was ready. Mohit got up. The girl was on the verge of tears. Nakul tried to console Mohit "Do not worry yaar…everything will be okay."

Satish asked Mohit, "Any… help?"

Mohit did not say anything. He just tried to smile; and moved towards his desk.

There was a newspaper on it with the headlines: Deadly cyclone ravages Orissa coast.

"Is it a must?"

"Yes dad…I have to go. But do not worry…everything there is okay now. I will keep you posted."

"But …he will get back to Delhi soon."

"We have already waited for a week pa, not a single phone call yet. I'm worried…and many other friends here…." Satish was looking at Selvi who was waiting outside the PCO. Nakul was standing next to her.

Rajaraman added hesitatingly, "Err….I hope nothing unfortunate had happened…." Satish knew his dad was just trying to be nice; just trying to keep his son comfortable.

The latest official figure of the death toll had crossed 9,000 – Nine thousand people. Puri was also hit badly. Some lucky ones there had been forced to move to safer locations before the cyclone unleashed its fury. Mohit was from Puri.

The 10 o'clock special train to Orissa looked like a long ship overloaded with a sea of disturbed human beings. A majority of them like – college students, politicians, old men, corporate staff, religious groups and jobless youth – were volunteers. Others were army men, hospital staff and the staff of some central government departments, representatives of foreign aid agencies and some NGOs. A few others were relatives of people who had been living – now, either dead or missing – in some coastal places in Orissa. A few were wailing beyond control. A few were numb to the chaos around them. Hardeep held Satish's hand tightly. The other two were too worried to say anything. Satish nodded while looking Hardeep in his eyes. Hardeep released his grip. Satish moved towards the other two and said, "Selvi, I will be back with Mohit." Selvi shook her head, while looking down. Her uncontrollable tears wetted the railway platform. Satish turned his head the other side. Nakul said in a low voice, "Take care buddy", while lifting Satish's bag that was on the ground. Satish collected the bag from him and got inside a coach.

He could not move beyond the wash basin that was behind the exit door of the coach. He turned back at his friends and waved just to say he was okay. Even before they could react some ten others squeezed themselves into the coach, hiding those three from Satish.

Satish was simply awestruck by what he saw. The whole area right outside the Bhubaneshwar railway station looked like a huge, assorted warehouse of relief items like rations, clothing, plastics sheets, light blankets, ORS packets, candles, chlorine tablets, match boxes, bleaching powder, biscuit packets and some medical kits. The ground was damp. The sky had many dark, microscopic eagles. The wind was calm. There were large army trucks. A specific place for the doctors and medical staff. Loudspeakers that constantly gave directions to people who were coming in thousands by train from many corners of the country. Journalists and TV camera men seeking statements on the situation. Police personnel trying hard to manage the crowd. And worst of all – a huge board with the names of towns and villages and – the corresponding number of casualties. A small tent was next to the board. There were eight people inside. While three of them were busy with the satellite phones, one fixed telephone lines and mobile phones. Four others were handling five fixed line telephones, a few registers, two computers, some maps and reams of papers. One was giving directions over the public address system. Only their civilian dresses assured him that it was not a war zone.

The whole area seemed chaotic, but every other minute loads of goods from trains were getting unloaded in an assembly line and reaching their allotted areas. Thirsty trucks were entering the premises for more men and material. One of Satish's co-passengers put him in an open van with relief material and a volunteer of Indian Red Cross Society, proceeding in the direction of Puri. Satish was made to sit on the top of a bundle of blankets. He felt very comfortable. There were also two nurses in the van. They had identity cards sound their necks. Satish opened the side zip of his bag to take out the chit with details like Mohit's address and his parents' names. He held tightly to the ropes provided on the sides of the van. The van continued its journey away from the capital.

The metalled road on which the van had started its journey was no more; it now was only a narrow path full of dislodged stones and orphaned tree branches.

At many places on the way Satish could see huge fires; a few people with their faces covered with handkerchiefs were near those mountains of fire that reached for the skies. Satish took time to realise the black smoke clouds had been playful calves and serene buffalos a week ago.

The van continued with its journey.

There was a cluster of tents at a spot on the roadside; on the other side of the tents were bunches of uprooted trees, two overflowing ponds and a queue of people in between the ponds. The tents were also overflowing with shocked survivors, helpless victims and selfless volunteers. Probably there were a few villages somewhere in the vicinity. "We would stop here for a few minutes." one of the nurses announced and got down from the van. Satish was still holding his bag tightly. He could just see a sea of terrified, blank looking survivors in front of him. He hesitated to get down. Images of the heaps of the dead and decaying cattle were still giving him nauseating feeling. He sat in the van holding on to his bag.

But he had over exerted himself over the last many hours since the night he boarded the train. He wanted to jump down and be comfortable for a while. Probably he would be able to have a cup of hot tea or some biscuits or at least some hot water. He got down. It started to drizzle.

Satish closed his eyes and looked up; he let the droplets of rain caress his face. But the noise and cries around him were disturbing. He moved near one of those tents.

It was a medical camp. A doctor was trying to calm down a hysterical woman; she had a baby in her arms. She wailed, wanting the doctor to attend her baby. A nurse was also helping the doctor in pacifying the unkempt woman. She even tried to hit the doctor who refused to attend her child. The queue outside that doctor's tent kept increasing. The doctor and the nurse struggled to keep the women in her senses but in vain. Many children punctuated the queue. But the woman would not move till the doctor looked at her baby. Satish watched what was happening. Even with so much noise around, the baby in her arms did not cry; it did not even bat an eyelid; did not move even its little finger.

Satish turned the other side and sat down holding one of those poles that supported the tent. The woman continued to curse the doctor for not attending to her baby.

"Catch him! Thief!!" Satish could hear someone shout. He looked. A young man was running away with some bundles of items that looked like medicines and biscuits. A few local people were seen chasing them. The lone policeman was whistling loudly. They jumped and disappeared behind the bushes. Satish tried to get up.

He moved towards the place where one of the nurses who had come along in the open van with him was busy sorting out some packets. Satish came and stood in front of her. She stopped her work and said, "We will move in some time." She asked Satish to have biscuits from the next tent. She gave him a couple of chlorine tablets. "Use it when you have water." He put them in his pant pocket.

Satish had some biscuits with hot water that was available. He opened the bag and went through the chit with Mohit's details for the nth time.

Their open van resumed its journey towards some place near Puri. One of the nurses had stayed back at the camp they had left. Another person had joined them. Satish could see things getting worse with every mile they covered. The sky was gloomy. Hundreds of huts and houses had turned to worthless piles of stones and wood. More and more fire mountains; more and more cattle carcasses on the sides of the path. The mother who would not accept it was only her child's body and not the child that was in her arms, refused to go from Satish's mind.

The van slowed down and stopped on the roadside. "Wait here on the main road. Vehicles to Puri would pass this place." Satish did not know how to thank them. He thought for a while and just said, "Thanks", and jumped from the van, holding his bag. The people in the van waved their and the nurse said, "May the Lord be with you." The van resumed its journey venting out big, jerky smoke bubbles. Satish stared at it till it disappeared. He took a full view of what was around him – uprooted trees, never-ending race of the reddish water to reach the lake-bunds, scattered rocks, floating fishes with silver bellies, huge branches separated from their motherly trunks, dark birds circling his head at a great height, two dead cows on the other side of the road, and – not even a single human being. He could hear only the sound of air passing gently near his ears.

No human voice. No thud of an engine. No sound of civilisation.

Satish looked around and chose the most comfortable-looking rock to sit upon. It was near an uprooted coconut tree. He opened his bag and reached for the pack of cigarette and matches. The cigarette was ready between his lips. He looked around aimlessly. Opened the matchbox. But he was not able to light the match stick. He tried hard. But his hands would not listen to him; they were too unsteady to scratch the match stick properly. He tried for some more time; but had to give up ultimately.

The wind seemed to blow with more vigour. He could hear women wailing. But he was not sure whether it was real or he imagined. "Will I ever be able to bury these memories?"

He was not comfortable being at one place. He stood up and walked down the road. The floating fishes glittered. He avoided looking at them. A few more steps. He felt the coconuts in the tree that was grounded now. He jumped over the cylindrical trunk and moved ahead. "It was Mohit's last attempt on IAS. Why now?" He walked. On reaching a swamp he stopped and turned around to walk back. He could hear the sound of a car at a distance. He felt relieved.

That was when it happened. Out of the thick bushes, out of nowhere, two men jumped and landed right in front of Satish. Satish was shocked to death. He stood speechless for a minute. Just a minute back he had felt he was miles away from human beings. And now two bony but intimidating men were bang in front of him. Even before he could react, one of them put a sharp weapon Satish's throat. Satish did not know what it was; but knew he was going to bleed to death now. The other one snatched Satish's bag. Satish could not even move his eyelids. Satish's heart beat filled the air. In no time they pushed Satish, and vanished; just the same way as they had appeared.

The impact of his fall brought Satish back to his senses; he got up quickly and cried out. Shouted. Abused them; first in Tamil, then in Hardeep's Hindi. He then picked big stones and threw it in the direction in which those two had fled. The sound of the car came to him. Satish was in the middle of the road, crying like a mad man. He shouted "Mohit!!... bastards!" It was unbearable. The minivan that was already packed with people of all kinds including an MLA, stopped some ten feet away from Satish. He was crying inconsolably. The people in the vehicle murmured something. The engine came to a rest. An old woman walked up to Satish and touched his head. Satish turned up. He could not see anything. He wiped off his tears; and started crying again. The old lady helped Satish to get up. He obliged, but was too weak to stand on his own. He tried to stop crying. He looked at the minivan. The lady hugged him. Satish broke down once again. The whole place reverberated with his cry.

The minivan stopped at the main relief camp, Puri. The town looked completely ruined. Everyone patted Satish before proceeding in different directions. The MLA gave Satish some cash and consoled him, "You will find him", before fading away with his men. Satish was like a machine – without any reaction. He was the last one to get down from the vehicle. He sat on the ground; with palms on his head. He did not move from the ground for the next half an hour. The place was full of activity. "Tell me address, address or family head's name…or even street name", the staff at the helpdesk counter in one of the tents told Satish. The staff got busy with the dozens others around him. Satish tried hard to recollect; he tried very hard. Nothing other than the word "Mohit" came to his mind. He tried. Nobody would believe this fellow had seen that chit with those details at least twenty times. He was not able to recollect even a single word from that chit, other than "Puri". Satish was losing sanity.

Satish came out of the tent and sat on the ground, again. He could not think or feel anything. An empty Gypsy approached the tent area at a high speed. It screeched to a halt and the driver rushed inside one of the tents. An announcement in the loudspeaker followed: "Attention please. Volunteers are needed urgently. Please come to the white Gypsy jeep that is waiting near tent no.4." The announcement repeated in English too. Gypsy started getting filled. It zoomed away once there was no more room left. Satish was the last one to get in.

After about fifteen minutes of travel it came to a halt. The people in Gypsy could sense a stench in the place even before they got down; Satish too could. He got an idea of what was it about. So did others. The Gypsy left in a jiffy, after dropping these volunteers. There were about five men, including two constables surrounding a police sub-inspector who was busy removing his uniform shoes. Satish and others joined them. Some planning and two hours later, this group of men was standing besides what they had pulled out from the swamp obstructed by cutoff branches and house rubbles – seventeen, half-decayed bodies; eight of them were children.

Satish was numb to anything in the outside world.

The Gypsy dropped them back at the main camp area.

Satish sat on the ground. He could not hear anything. He closed his eyes.

There was an increased level of activity in the camp area. Most of them were moving to tent no.7. The loudspeakers seemed to be requesting people to do so. The loudness gradually pulled Satish also. He too joined the people outside tent no.7. There was a man in safari, standing on a desk outside the tent. His swollen eyes said he had not slept in the recent past. Around fifty people had gathered there. Satish was not able to stand and spotted a broken chair in a corner; he sat delicately. The man in safari spoke something for the next 5 minutes. Satish could not figure out what it was about. He could only guess it was in Oriya. But the speech commanded Satish's attention. His ears could clearly hear every word spoken. His heart could feel the message. His eyes watched the way every word was created; the gestures that gave a ray of hope; the confidence that began to spread in air. The man finished his speech with "Jai Hind!" All others joined him in chorus.

He jumped from the desk and quickly walked to his car. People followed him. The PA opened him the door of the red-beaconed Ambassador.

Satish asked the man next to him, "Who?" pointing to the Ambassador car. He replied, "Shiv Prasad sir. Head of the relief work here... IAS officer." The old, horrible Ambassador picked speed.

PART V: CHANGE OF SEASON

"You need not come to the classes for the next few days. I will send across the notes..." Rao came closer to Satish, held his hands and looked into his eyes and said, "I am proud of you, son." Satish remembered his father. Rao's eyes were moist. Satish felt embarrassed and looked out of the window; the balcony door on the other side was closed, as usual. Hardeep was thrilled. So was every one of the 380-odd students with AIC. Nobody could have even imagined that Rao would take all the efforts to meet someone who never cared for IAS or anything connected to it. Hardeep and Satish walked down the stairs of the apartment to see off Rao; Satish too did not even dream of Rao climbing up the three floors to meet this hopeless, rogue.

Satish had reached Delhi two days back; Selvi had not come out of her room since meeting Satish the day he reached Delhi.

Nakul and Satish took great pains to compel the reclusive Selvi to be out of her room – at least once in three days. She sometimes took her books to Mohit's room and studied there for a while before breaking down and heading back to her room. Nakul could just be a mute spectator during those times.

After a few days of piling up the class notes delivered at home Satish was back in the classroom; at his allotted seat in the first row. Some still envied him. Many started liking him.

Satish and Nakul took out Selvi on two successive Sundays to Ulan Bator. Egg fried rice and chicken Manchurian. Satish tried to console Selvi, "I'm sure everything is fine there…he will be here any moment." But only the ravages of cyclone came to his mind when he was saying that. He could see the smoke clouds; hear the piercing wails; the stench of decaying bodies. He could also feel that sharp weapon on his throat.

Selvi could not feel hope in Satish's words.

December 1999. The last month of the century. The world was gearing up for the first minute of the twenty-first century. Old Rajinder Nagar was also charged up. But it was mainly for a different reason. Temples, churches and other places of worship saw a spike in the young crowd; it was due to those students who prayed for God's generous blessings for the next 17 months or so. The notification for the UPSC Civil Services Exams was out in all major newspapers. The Preliminary Examination (Prelims) would be in another six months, on May 14, 2000; the final rank list would be out in a year after that, in May 2001. The Mains Exam and the interview were in between.

Civil service aspirants started queuing up in the post offices where the forms were available. Naturally, Rajinder Nagar post office had a tough time managing the crowd. Even though the last date of application was many weeks away, and the availability of the forms was never an issue many students thronged the application form counters on the first day itself. Probably it has got something to do with the *kick* one gets on watching a film the first day of its release. Satish was at his allotted seat. Rao was engrossed in explaining, in his typical style that blended hand movements and facial expressions to produce a dramatic effect, some of the interesting case studies of Freud. Rao would need one more lecture to complete the chapter on mental disorders and therapies. He usually finished the whole syllabus by the end of March so that the students had one full month to prepare themselves for the May Prelims.

Some students got uncomfortable in the class when Rao described a few aspects of Freud's approach to personality and disorders. There were giggles, sometimes. However many others felt the Freudian concepts on basic human drives were adding spice to their otherwise boring life filled with books, exams and tasteless food. Satish too enjoyed the classes on Freud.

The Prelims application form was a very simple data sheet asking for basic details like name, educational qualification, address, etc and the choice of the optional subject in which the candidate wished to appear. Sometimes one could not believe that this single sheet was the application form for the mind-boggling Exam that increased the candidates' age by minimum one year.

The necessary details were supposed to be shaded using an HB pencil in the appropriate boxes. The optional paper for Prelims ranged from electrical engineering to anthropology. Some of the students even went to the Dholpur House, the office building of Union Public Service Commission, in groups and lined up for the application forms there. They felt it would bring them some luck and directly take them to the interview day. Hardeep was one of such candidates. An acknowledgement postcard accompanied the application form. One needed to fill in one's own postal address in that post card, send it to UPSC along with the filled-up application form and wait for the card's return with the UPSC seal.

At one of the teashops outside the UPSC one could see groups of students with brand new application forms in their hands. While having tea, most of them cursed their luck in the previous attempts; some of them regretfully informed others that it was their last attempt and they did not know what to do if they failed even that time. A few also expressed disbelief on the previous year's results that had instantaneously turned their seemingly brainless friends – into famous and powerful IAS and IPS officers. "The selection has to be more objective…and less painful", that seemed to be the loudest statement in the tea stall.

Hardeep returned from Dolphur House with three application forms. Even during his earlier attempt, he had gone to UPSC buildings for the application form.

"Yes…but I don't know why they are all thrilled", Satish's voice reached Kumar in Madurai through the STD-ISD PCO. He continued, "Harry got me the form…I still could not believe that I'm going to appear in the I-A-S exams!!"

Kumar laughed and asked, "What is your dad saying?"

"What else?…jumping with joy! But I don't know what that mad man is going to do…he told me some surprise is waiting for me this New Year day… I hope he does not take me to the President or someone like that!"

Kumar laughed again, "You never know!"

Though Satish was fully aware of what was happening, he could not believe what he was doing. Hardeep and Selvi were also there, in Satish's room that had two new wooden racks overloaded with GS and psychology books. Satish was holding an HB pencil. A ball pen and the application form were on his desk. "What is this joke going on!" Only his college and school days came to his mind. He felt like laughing; he realised he was wasting others time as well; he concluded he was making a fool of himself.

Satish was shading the tiny boxes provided for the choice of optional paper in the application form. He shaded the number 17; it stood for psychology. For a moment he remembered how he landed up with psychology as his optional paper. Hotel Royal Prince; Mohit; Rao's classes; the seventeen decaying bodies; and Shiv Prasad IAS.

Satish was no more allergic to the three letters I, A and S; in fact, in some corner of his heart – he was feeling proud to be filling the form.

The Prelims form was complete with Satish's signature and the date with it. No sooner did he finish writing 12.12.99, there was applause. Satish was surprised initially; later totally embarrassed. Selvi and Hardeep were clapping teasingly. In the fifty-plus years history of the IAS exams nobody had ever got a clapping for merely filling the Prelims application form.

The claps also made everyone forget Mohit's absence, for a while.

Satish did not sleep that afternoon. Hardeep mesmerised Satish with *"Hey ajnabee, tu bhi kabhi..."* and left Satish's room to resume his studies of heat transfer, refrigeration and air conditioning; it was supposed to be an important topic under the syllabus for mechanical engineering optional. Satish could still hear those lines even two minutes after Hardeep had locked his room from inside and started studying. In a way the song also created a perfect mood for Satish's nap, but he tried very hard and kept awake. Satish smoked for a while and when left with nothing else – he even browsed his psychology notes. He found the classes on motivation, personality and creativity interesting. He could clearly remember every word Rao had spoken in those classes; he also remembered the dramatic and funny gestures Rao had made during the lectures. "I wish I had a teacher like this during school days!" Satish often told himself during those times when he tried to rationalise his Madurai flash-back.

After a while Satish reached Tinku's tea shop. Satish was having the filled application form in his hand. Tinku looked happy as there was not much crowd for tea; his tender hands were not aching. But the shop would be get choked with candidates in another 15 minutes when the afternoon batches of the coaching classes got over. Satish looked a little disappointed. He got a cigarette and was about to light it when someone snatched the cigarette from behind. The crushed, live cigarette landed in the dustbin amidst empty tea cups, *gutka* covers and thoroughly used tea powder. "Oh…I thought you got late!" Satish said in a meek attempt to justify that cigarette. He pitied the cigarette that did not get a chance to realise its talent. "I was at the book shop. Did you read the latest issue of Yojana?" Selvi asked; disgustingly looking at the dustbin. She thought for a while and said, "Okay…sir will get free in some time. We can wait in the office"

Both of them proceeded towards the AIC building. The clerk smiled at them before resuming with his work of sorting out the fresh load of study material. They got seated in those chairs outside Rao's cabin. *"2 selections in Top 10 in 1999 results"*. The notice board was right in front of them. For a moment Satish imagined his photo being there among those tiny photos in the brochure. "How foolish of me!!" He turned away from the notice board to look at Selvi, whose sad eyes were still staring at the notice board.

The lecture hall door opened. Rao came out. The noisy herd of aspirants rushed after him. A few followed him to his cabin. Satish and Selvi stood when he crossed them. But Rao was too busy with his thoughts to have a look at these two. "It is going to take another 15 minutes before these over-enthu people came out", Satish quipped referring to those students who were in a constant need of some personal interaction with the teacher. Selvi gave an affectionate knock on Satish's head and said, "Keep quiet…they are sincere students, not like you!"

The few students who went in asked Rao many a doubt – some relevant, many irrelevant for the exam. For the relevant ones Rao gave clear explanations and ensured that the basic concepts stayed with the candidates for their life. For questions like, "Sir, what use of studying optionals like history, anthropology etc…? I just want to be an IPS Officer" Rao invariably was curt with his reply, "Don't waste my time. Go and ask that to the UPSC chairman." Rao took a sip of water. All the students had gone out after getting their doubts cleared. Selvi and Satish got in. Rao smiled and said, "Please sit." Selvi took out the filled application form; Satish also did the same.

"We need your blessings sir", said Selvi handing over the form to Rao. Satish also nodded and copied Selvi's action. Rao was happy when he got the forms. He glanced the forms, one after the other, and said, "I know the efforts you put in Selvi…am sure you will pass with flying colours this time! The country needs officers like you!" The slight sadness in Rao's eyes said he missed Mohit. Rao was not even sure whether Mohit was appearing in the exam or not. Some months back Rao had been sure that Mohit too would be on their notice board, among the top 10 selections that year; but was shocked when he got to know about Mohit's interview marks that threw him out of the list. Looking at Satish, Rao had convincingly said, "I'm sure you will be an IAS soon.....I know your potential." Satish had smiled and thanked Rao for his nice words.

Actually Satish felt like telling him, "Sir, have a talk with my school HM...he will tell you about my real potential!"

The last dawn of the second millennium. Satish had been struggling for quite a few weeks now to wake up on time for the 10 o' clock classes. His smoking had gone up over the past few weeks and he regularly had a peg of brandy at night – mostly just before crashing. It was only with extreme difficulty that he threw his quilt aside and managed to get up from the cot, everyday. He had paid the landlord Rs.400 more for using the room heater. During the day he felt very heavy and uncomfortable. Starting with the VIP Bonus white banian and topping up with the dirty red jerkin, he wore a minimum of four layers of garments. A T-shirt and a thick red sweater with the caption "Everlast" embroidered in black came in between; on some days a thermal as well.

But for during his Kodaikkanal trips Satish had not experienced chillness below 25 degree C. On some days his father had advised him, "It is very cold these days. Use the thick blanket during the nights", as the previous night's temperature might have touched 22 degree C. Right from the December-end one could see morning walkers in Madurai use full sleeved sweaters; and mufflers round their head. Some of them even postponed their walk by an hour and started at 7 AM – apparently to protect them from the imaginary cold wave that brought down the town's temperature to almost 20 degree C in the early mornings. Satish enjoyed prolonging his sleep during such days.

The minimum temperature would have touched 3 degree C that early morning; Satish switched off the alarm twice before getting up finally around 9:30 AM. Satish had stopped taking breakfast during these cold days. He felt sleeping a bit longer on an empty stomach was more bearable than rising earlier in the winter mornings to fill the stomach with those *idli*-like items. However the major plus point for Satish during winters was that one was not obliged to take bath daily. His average, with much difficulty, was – thrice a week. So he hardly took more than 20 minutes to be at the first row, after having a cup of Tinku's special tea. Tinku worked over-time during winters.

It was another day of boring lecture for Satish. It was the final class on Indian polity. Rao was covering the Schedules, and some important Amendments to the Constitution. Satish found only the psychology optional classes interesting. GS, especially the topics under polity and history bored him. Even after about 70 days of IAS preparation Satish had a difficult time recollecting the Fundamental Rights in the sequence given in our Constitution. But compared to his college days he was infinitely better off, as he would not have been able to even differentiate between the Independence Day and the Republic Day then. "Any more doubts?" Rao asked his customary question before ending the lecture. One of them from the corners raised a Cello pen and asked, "Sir, can the President veto a Constitutional Amendment Bill?"

Satish was happy he was able to guess the right answer for that question.

"Go through these polity notes thoroughly…you will be able to score at least 50 marks under this section. We will be moving to statistics tomorrow…er…the day after tomorrow. Tomorrow will be a holiday. Use the time to revise. Happy new year, new millennium…may your dreams come true this year!" The whole class responded in chorus, "Happy new year sir!" Rao smiled and left. The mood of celebration filled the entire classroom. "Happy Y2K!" the girl sitting next to Satish wished him. She had a beaming smile. Satish also took the opportunity to wish and even shake hands with a few other fair girls. He was thrilled; but not as much as he would have been a few weeks back. He was also hungry. "May be I could ask her out for the new year's party." Satish walked down the road kicking the empty tea cup. He shifted to a small, round stone once the cup got crushed beyond shape. The round stone cooperated better with Satish and he was able to dribble it till his apartment when he finally kicked it hard towards the imaginary goal post on the wall on the other side of the road.

Satish went to Selvi's room on way to the evening psychology classes. The room door was open; she was hidden behind a few books and registers. Satish felt a bit uneasy as he felt he was disturbing her studies.

"Hey come in! How are you doing?"

"Fine, just on the way to the psycho class…" Satish told her, a little hesitatingly.

"How is it going?" she asked looking at the books that were lying scattered all over the place.

"Not bad…very boring!"

Selvi smiled. She looked down at the books on her desk.

"Okay… I will go for the class. Bye! Bye! Take care" Satish left her room. He had not met Hardeep for the post-lunch session. Hardeep's door was locked. Satish wanted to talk with someone. He rushed towards Tinku's hoping to pass time there.

Selvi continued with her studies.

Rao explained Stockholm Syndrome in an interesting way with many incredible case studies. Satish was engrossed in the lecture on the psychology of terrorism that formed an important topic of paper two of psychology optionals. Unlike the GS classes Satish had some friends in the psychology class. They invariably discussed the lecture and revised the key topics at Tinku's after classes, before heading home for dinner. Satish also provided an element of fun in those discussions. After the lecture on creativity Satish proudly told others how he had used the best of his creative potential on April Fool's day many years back.

Satish even gave some smart answers in a few psychology classes. Rao felt proud.

"Tomorrow will be a holiday. Use the time to revise. Happy new year, new millennium...May your dreams come true this year!" Rao finished the lecture. Satish remembered the New Year days of The Desperados times. "It was heaven!"

He did not stop at Tinku's for the discussion; he walked to the nearby PCO. He tried Mohit's Orissa number; he got the same message that he had been getting for the past few weeks – the number did not exist. Then Satish dialed his father's number. After hearing the DSR with a special emphasis on the Old Rajinder Nagar weather report his father excitedly asked Satish, "New year party plans?" Satish was quite irritated. "To become an IAS officer" he said and hung the phone up.

Students, young men, uncles and retired people pushed one another alike to reach the counter. The shop had deputed two over-sized men to handle the New Year crowd. There was literally a fight for the bottles. The mob in front of the liquor shop simply stunned Satish. "But where did this Harry fellow go?!" Satish had no clue as to how he was going to celebrate the new millennium that was to be born in a matter of about another three hours. Satish too joined the crowd. But soon lost interest in the quarrel for alcohol and resumed his walk to his room. He remembered his glorious days back home. He had never even dreamt that he might be finding it difficult to buy something as simple as a Kalyani.

Famous Fruit Juice was also overflowing with life, mainly college students and civil service aspirants. Satish could see many pairs; he had seen some of those faces in his GS class. Attractive banners and serial bulb patterns welcomed the new millennium. Most of the shops had "Special 2000 price". The sporadic sounds of fire crackers added to the usual noise of the place. Diwali rockets occasionally illuminated the polluted, dark sky. Some loudspeakers kept on the roadside were shouting at the top of their voices. The kids in Bullets were speeding merrily, noisily. Tinku's teashop was closed. Hotel Royal Prince was full. Vijay was busy.

Satish continued his walk. Out of nowhere a bike stopped in front of him. Satish took a few moments to recognise who it was. "Happy 2000 *sirji*", Navin greeted Satish in his typical way. His bike zoomed. There was a lady with him.

Satish kicked hard the weak stray dog that was sleeping outside his apartment. The dog cursed him before running away. Satish was totally blank while climbing the stairs. He lit a Milds. He hoped that Hardeep was in the room. He opened the flat's door and rightaway looked at Hardeep's room. "Thank God! He is here." Satish gave a sigh of relief. He then picked his dinner packet up from the main door latch and got inside the flat. "I hope he is not going to study tonight also." He locked the flat's door from inside and turned towards his room. Satish could not believe what he saw. "Is this a dream?!" Three items were kept in front of his room door. Satish picked them up and shouted happily. Two Kalyani Black Label bottles and a pack of Malabar chips from Madurai.

Satish started flying with joy. He quickly went to Hardeep's room.

He knew who was there. He banged on the door shouting, "You buggers!" One could hear Hardeep's laughter before the door opened and Kumar came out. Satish shrieked and hugged him. His joy crossed all limits. His eyes turned moist.

"No Sat, you guys please carry on..." Hardeep insisted that he would stay back in the flat. "You are a boring bastard Harry!" Satish pushed him into his room and came out of the flat with Kumar. Hardeep shut the door and resumed his studies. Kumar was shivering occasionally, due to the Delhi winter. Both of them simultaneously lit cigarettes with the same match stick. Satish stopped an auto rickshaw. Kumar could not believe his eyes and ears when he saw Satish bargain with the auto *rickshawala*. "Hindi?!!" Kumar asked Satish as soon as they sat in the rickshaw. Satish proudly pulled up the thick collars of his dirty jerkin and replied, "Yeah! *Kuchuu kuchhu aata hai!*"

Red signal. Auto rickshaw stopped. "I'm really scared boss..." Kumar continued with a serious tone, "...there are so many books in your room. Your flat-mate also says you are a very sincere student! I can't believe it! I simply can't believe it Mr.Gang leader!" Kumar ended his statement in an excited voice; and with a little difficulty as the ice cold air was hitting his face like an ice water jet. Satish took a few seconds and quipped very seriously, "Of course, yes! You should feel proud that you are sitting next to a future IAS topper!" and raised his head and blew-out smoke that hit the roof of the auto rickshaw. Realising the counter-attack Kumar said in no time, "Sorry mate! Luck will not take you that far!" before both of them broke into a laughter. The auto rickshaw stopped. They had reached Connaught Place.

Both of them were amazed. They had not seen such a grand New Year celebration in their lives. CP was glittering with bright lights of all colours; the euphoric crowd waited cheerfully for the clock to strike 12. Only ten more minutes between the world and the Y2K. Many were singing and dancing in small groups on the wide roads. Loud film numbers and soap bubbles filled the air. Gigantic florescent balloons with "Hello Y2K" printed on them pierced the low clouds. Live bands performed in the parking lots and small road junctions. Oversized TV screens were beaming images from the eastern side of the globe where the sun's rays of the new millennium had already kissed the planet. Shining ribbons and serial bulb sets were coiled around the huge white pillars of the buildings. Colourful confetti too added more joy to the celebration. The safe return of the hostages from Afghanistan had infused fresh energy into the millennium revelry.

Kumar pinched himself to ensure that it was not a dream. He could not believe that such fair girls actually existed outside the silver screen. "This is nothing…just wait for some more time. You will go mad," Satish pepped Kumar up like a local tourist guide. Kumar did not even blink for minutes together; he did not want to miss anything, anyone. Some had not overly-covered themselves with jerkins, shawls or sweaters. Kumar's eyes quickly scanned the area and accurately focused on such women. The duo stopped at a liquor shop and Satish managed to get a full-bottle of Old Monk. He gulped twice from the 1.5L Pepsi PET bottle he had and poured some rum into it until it was full. Then both of them took big gulps from the Pepsi bottle; that was enough to empty the Monk into it. Kumar threw the empty Monk on the lamppost at a distance and loudly appealed "Howwzzz thaatt?!" Satish, with a stiff upper lip, nodded and raised his right hand with the index finger pointing upwards. They laughed like mad men after that. The sound of the bottle shattering was feeble compared to the voice of celebration. Satish was shaking the PET bottle while they walked towards more noisy areas.

For a moment all the loud speakers kept quiet. Satish and Kumar looked at each other. Kumar took a sip from the Pepsi bottle and tried to figure out what had happened. *"Ten, nine, eight, seven…."* A thunderous, euphoric mixture of many voices and loud speakers tore all ears with "Happy New Year!!"

Bright streaks and fountains of coloured stars filled the dark sky. The sound of crackers that followed continued for another half an hour into the new millennium. Every corner of CP and every face there was visible as if one thousand lightnings stayed in the sky up above. Satish and Kumar wished and hugged each other. The loud music had become louder after the countdown. The roadside dances became wilder. More police men got down from the patrol vehicles. Many sweaters, blazers, shawls and jerkins were lying scattered on the grass in a corner of Central Park that had turned into an open air discotheque. Huge loudspeakers were placed on tall stands. The place was lit with the usual sodium vapour bulbs and a few coloured bulbs specially arranged for the event. Most of the dancing men and women were drenched in sweat. It was a cold winter night.

Satish and Kumar joined the dancing crowd. Satish shouted "Hoo…Hooooo!!" while the empty Pepsi bottle flew. Many couples found dark corners to continue their dance. The film numbers were getting louder, and faster. It was one full hour into the year 2000.

"That one", Kumar winked at Satish and pointed to a very tall and fair girl in a jet-black top and long, dark skirt. They moved closer to her. Satish was engrossed in the music. His dance steps were as untamed as the loud beats in the background. Two other men were dancing with that fair girl in black dress. Kumar was not able to balance his body perfectly; but he managed some peculiar dance movements without falling down. Cigarette smoke engulfed the whole place like early morning fog. A few rockets were still illuminating the skyline. Satish's dirty red jerkin was on the ground. He was dancing on it.

In a while these two had joined the other two men and danced around that girl, who seemed to be in a different world. A rocket that lit the sky showed the reduced distance between these four men and the girl in the centre. Asha Bhosle was singing *"rangeela re..."* very beautifully; loudly. Kumar kept his gaze fixed on the girl while they danced. He picked a cigarette from Satish's pocket and lit it. Satish's steps unfailingly matched the beats that seemed to get faster. The girl in the centre was dancing with her hands reaching out to the sky. She also screamed occasionally. The other two men were also lost in dance. After some time, one of them said "Brother" and pulled the cigarette out of Kumar's mouth; Kumar was busy staring at the girl. The wet hair added to her glamour.

That person took a few puffs. The cigarette passed hands; went in a circle and reached him again only as a butt; it had also passed through the centre of the circle. Kumar saw the leftover of the cigarette and was a little surprised. Satish offered one more cigarette to Kumar. He lit it. The loud beats made everyone continue dancing hysterically. There were infrequent sounds crackers. After taking a deep puff, Kumar said "Please madam" and directly passed the smoking cigarette to the centre of the circle.

For the next few moments Kumar could not hear even the

deafening beats of *"Chaiyya chaiyya..."* or see anyone dancing. He could only feel stars inside his head and hear only a long, sharp beep tone. A heavy punch had landed on his chin. Though Kumar did not fall, by the time he took to stabilise he could see Satish sitting over one of the other men and punching him nonstop with both the fists. The fair lady was not around. The backdrop of the loud music persisted. Others were busy dancing in their own worlds. The other man wrenched Satish's neck from behind with his elbow. Kumar went and kicked him from behind. But he turned and gave Kumar another severe blow that broke one of his front teeth. That person turned to Satish again and continued to tighten the grip on his neck. Satish still managed to punch the fellow on whom he was sitting. The numbers were also getting wilder.

About fifteen others stopped their dance and turned to cheer the fight. Kumar did not feel any pain. He scrambled the ground for a while; there were only a few wet jackets. He took some more time and ultimately laid his hands on a piece of garden hose. The other man still had a grip on Satish's neck. Kumar got up and swirled the hose twice before shouting, "Take this bastard!" and landing it from behind on the face of the one gripping Satish's neck. He fell down yelling louder than the loud speakers. By then Satish had broken the nose; and three teeth of the person who had punched Kumar.

The audience around them had grown to thirty. They were loud.

Within a short time the noise of a police whistle was approaching the crowd. The dancing crowd on the other side too got alert. Satish got up quickly and pulled Kumar's shirt while clearing the way with his other hand. Many eyes were on them. Many girls screamed. The other two who were injured were still struggling to get up. The crowd was set to disperse as the constables approached them. Satish was shouting "Fast! Fast!" while moving out and pushed one of the huge speakers kept on a tall stand; it landed with a heavy thud; the beats were softer for a moment and the music completely went-off after that. It was messy. Everyone in the crowd started rushing out of the place without caring for their leather jackets and other winter-wear which lay scattered on the ground. Some of the cars had already started to move out of the parking lots. Many bikes zoomed out. Police toppled a few of them by throwing their *lathis* on the bike wheels. No more music. Only screams and police whistles.

Satish almost reached the other end of the crowd when he picked up an empty beer bottle from the ground and threw it at the metal shutter of a closed shop far away. The sound of glass shattering sent a chill down many spines; more and more bikes raced out. Police rushed in from many sides of the Central Park.

Satish and Kumar ran along with many others for about half a kilometre and stood gasping. They could hear police whistles and accelerating cars and bikes at a distance. Satish pulled Kumar and ran for another few hundred metres before coming to halt near a bright bus stop. They walked further ahead to reach a dark zone and turned towards the wall to pull down their trouser zippers. Looking at each other they shouted in sync, "Happy Y2K!"

PART VI: NEW MILLENNIUM

The same old New Delhi railway station. "But I really feel you have decided to become an IAS" Kumar said in a low voice while holding his chin with the left hand. His face was swollen. "Come on dumbo! Don't go by what Harry says. He is just trying to boost me. He is from IIT and last year even he failed to clear this exam! And the books you see in my room…I did not go and buy them. That fellow Mohit got them for me. He is such a nice guy, you know…and what I saw in Orissa..." Satish stopped his reply midway while lifting Kumar's shoulder bag and suitcase. The train to Jaipur would be leaving in another few minutes. Like a defence lawyer cornering a witness, Kumar asked "Oh…that means you want to become an I.A.S. officer, but you don't think you are capable enough?!" Satish took time and looking at the train signal said, "Board the train before it reaches Jaipur." Kumar continued while they were entering the coach, "Even …Naidu…er…Reddy….no no…Rao sir… of that institute had come to your room…someone delivered class notes at your room daily!!" "That was for something else, stupid" Satish retorted. Satish pushed the luggage below the seat when they reached the fourth bay of the coach. Kumar had to meet an important customer in Jaipur. "Even the girl who came to wish you a happy new year…Selvi…yeah, she too gave you a good conduct certificate!! But I can't take that! Impossible!" Kumar sat down and continued in spite of the horrible pain in and around his mouth, "…as if all this were not enough, the first row seat!! How can you do that?! How?!" With much difficulty and overcoming the pain on his face, Kumar managed to laugh like a hyena. The other passengers around them looked at him strangely. Satish smiled and put his hand on Kumar's shoulder and said, "Come on…I am still the same…you saw it during the new year…" The train started to move. Kumar and Satish walked towards the exit. Satish got down. Groups of people in the platform were waving at the departing train. Kumar raised his voice and in a serious tone, "Okay…but what about this?..." and continued without waiting for Satish's reply, "…Till now you have not spoken even a single word about Maharaja 2005." Kumar nodded and continued, "…that is good. Keep going…I'm proud of you!"

The train picked speed. Satish walked faster. Kumar shouted, "Bye, bye!!...Satish I.A.S"

Many more days passed. There were frequent cold waves. There were even days when the dense fog turned everyone almost blind. Many aspirants found it impossible to stay awake and prepare in the nights. They changed their study schedule to be in line with the harsh season. It was bone chilling. Hardeep had a bottle of beer every third day as his body machine needed frequent oiling. Satish joined him occasionally. Smoking worked better for Satish. He had paid that extra Rs.400 to the landlord. But the room heater did not help him much and during the nights only Satish's head protruded out of the heavy quilt. It was 1:20 AM. Satish was getting used to winters.

Satish did not know what was really happening to him. He was feeling confused and quite disturbed, since Kumar's New Year visit. Satish was again caught in a web of complex emotions. For many days Kumar's parting words haunted him many times over. He could still not come to terms with it. "But why did Kumar say that? Do I really want to become Satish I.A.S?! Don't kid yourself, Satish." He could only marvel at the way his life had changed course in Delhi. He remembered everything that had happened since the day he had reached Delhi. He also remembered every word spoken by Rao after his return from Orissa. Satish felt happy about the way others respected him. In one corner of his mind he also was worried about Mohit. "What happened to that poor chap? My first guru." Satish could hear the whistle of the security man on the streets. It was 3 o' clock. "I should also make my father proud. This whole thing was that foolish man's dream." The Madurai Collectorate episode flashed in his mind. The people waiting to meet the District Collector; the kind of respect a Collector commands came to his mind. Without any reason his mind went to his college director-owner's room. "Are you not ashamed to have brought up a son like this?" Satish could remember his father falling at the feet of Mr.Sakthivel; he could also clearly see the tears in his father's eyes.

A few dogs were howling below his apartment. They stopped Satish's confusion for a moment. Just for a moment. "Preparing for the IAS is not just the hare-tortoise story…Rao should be kidding. No…but it can actually be that way…" Satish was going mad again. Three months back it was about how to pass one year's time in that mad and boring world of IAS Exam preparation. Three months back he was concerned only with Maharaja 2005. Now it was something else totally. The decaying corpses, the mother with the dead child, the sharp object on his throat and the cries came to his mind. It was 4 AM. "Yes… Shiv Prasad sir!! Can I be like him?"

Since the first day of the millennium Satish had been cursing Kumar for confusing him. And it invariably spoilt his night sleep. Satish also remembered Hardeep's sweet voice that had made him sleep well in the afternoons. His mind jumped to the classroom. "I'm sure you will be an IAS soon…..I know your potential" Rao's words flashed in his mind.

It was close to 5AM. The scene of his father seeing him off at the Madras Central railway station with moist eyes came before his eyes. Fog blanketed the whole area that day also. All of a sudden Satish pushed the heavy quilt aside and quickly got up from the cot. He switched on the lights and opened the shelf in a hurry. He reached for something in the drawer and put it on the desk. It was the two-line note his father had sent during his initial Delhi days; those days when Satish was a hopeless refugee in this jungle of books and IAS aspirants. "Dear Satish, God bless you. Hope you remember what I told you at the Madras railway station. I'm sure you will make me proud. Love, Father".

Satish quickly grabbed the ball pen lying on the desk and wrote below the lines his father had written. "I promise, I will."

He thought for a moment and stylishly signed: *R.Satish I.A.S.*

The bulky India Year Book 2000 was wide open on Satish's desk; the pages were flapping in the fan breeze. The GS class register was below the book. The white light from Lakshman Sylvania filled the entire room. The digital timepiece on the desk showed: 01:33 AM. 14 Mar 2000. Two thin books were lying on the floor, to the right side of the chair. They had the previous years' question papers for GS and psychology. Cigarette butts filled both the ash trays kept on the desk. To the left, on the floor, were the latest copies of *Yojana* and *Frontline*. The two book racks did not have space even for one more sheet of paper. A 2-foot pile of the previous two months' newspapers was below the window. An Oxford Advanced Learner's dictionary acted as a paper weight.

A 3' X 4' white sheet of thermacol was fixed on the wall, just above the desk. The thermacol had a few newspaper clippings with the highlights of Railway Budget 2000-20001, key economic data and some sports statistics pinned to it. A piece of paper with words like Gardner, Cattel, Spearman, Goleman etc was pinned to the bottom of the sheet on the right side. A State Bank of India calendar for the year 2000 hung from the right door of the cupboard. On the left door, just below the *Bhaghavad Gita* sticker, cellophane tapes held the Kodaikkanal photo of The Desperados tightly.

Satish was on the chair; sleeping with his head resting on the latest newspaper lying on the desk.

Some of his new clothes were lying among the piles of worn out clothes in the hall. Many clothes looked like the canvas used by a chimpanzee for modern art paintings. Satish was made to celebrate Holi a few days back. Though The Desperados had also played their part during Holi by spraying fountain pen ink on innocent front-benchers and lecturers, what Satish saw here was just beyond his imagination. "What a way to celebrate Holi!" He was simply bowled over by the way people enjoyed the festival of colours. "These are the crucial days…do not go out and waste time. Holi comes every year." Hardeep's warning had made Satish focus on the chapters an Attitude and Emotions in their psychology syllabus. Initially, Satish did feel bad that his friend did not allow him to play Holi. But soon he too realised the exams were just round the corner and it was good to forget the festival. However a few children from the neighbourhood had barged into their flat to give Satish a first-hand *real* Holi experience. Those clothes have been lying in the hall since then.

In another fifty days over one lakh candidates across the country would be appearing in two, two-hour objective exams – Prelims. Sunday. 14th May 2000. The forenoon session was for the GS paper. Optional subjects were after lunch. These four hours would decide whether Satish would be in the list of around 5000 candidates, who would get a chance to appear in the Mains exam in October.

The tiny timepiece cried. 1:35AM. Satish woke up with a sudden jerk. He closed the Year Book and picked a thin book lying on the floor, to his right. It had the solved GS Prelims question papers since the year 1990.

"It's going to be out anytime today...probably post-lunch sometime..." Two weeks to go for Prelims 2000. "No chance!! The rumours about the result have been circulating for the past ten days...today is just another day." This was the usual time when the final selection list of the exams conducted the previous year was declared. Everyone in the Old Rajinder Nagar was geared up for the results. So was the entire country. Thousands of candidates were eagerly looking forward to the results that gave them some sort of inspiration. Even Tinku was anxious.

But the most restless lot was the candidates who had given the interview a month back corresponding to the Prelims of the year 1999. In no way could they be sure that they would find a place in the final list; so they had to be ready for the Prelims 2000 that was just a stone's throw away. But with the thoughts of the results filling up their hearts and heads they could in no way sit, revise and ready themselves for the oncoming Prelims. Taking the exam without a proper revision and the right frame of mind also meant wasting one more attempt. "Why can't they give out the results at least one month before the Prelims...this is the heights of sadism", that was the statement uttered most often at the Famous Fruit Juice. Some candidates felt that was like the Election Commission asking the contestants to get on with the full-fledged campaigns for the next elections, even before the results of the previous elections were announced. The IAS results drama stressed out even the calmest ones among the aspirants. Rumours were generated on a daily basis, some days on an hourly basis too. "Someone from Himachal has topped the exam", "You know they have increased the selection list to 515", "An LIC agent has topped this time.", "The results are going to be announced only after the Prelims." The rumours came and went in various shapes and colours.

The UPSC had decided to declare the final selection list that day. It was 1130 AM. The news was all over the place and the country. Mr.Sorabh Babu Maheshwari, an IIT graduate, was the happiest person that day. He stood first. All India Rank, AIR 001.

One could hear a pin drop. Selvi was also present in that special session. It has been a practice at the AIC to conduct a short "war cry" session exactly a week before the Prelims. Rao believed, while his regular lectures armed the aspirants with knowledge, the final, special session made them pull the trigger when it mattered – May 14th 2000. The lecture hall was jam-packed. There was also a special energy in the air as four of AIC's candidates had found a place in the AIR top ten of the final selections. While waiting for Rao to start the session, most of the aspirants were seen revising some topics from the handwritten notes they had prepared. Such notes had the key points from the subjects; and lots of mnemonic codes to help one remember tons of facts. Satish was at his usual seat in the first row. The little chit of paper in his hand had the summary of the chapter: Final days of freedom struggle. He was also revising.

An energetic Rao quickly entered the room. All others closed their books and turned towards him. Rao glanced at the whole class. He could see eyes filled with hope and fear; with confidence and anxiety. There was a long pass. Rao did not utter a word, but just grabbed a white board marker. Satish resembled someone in a deep penance. Fully focused. He, like everyone else in the lecture room, knew what passing the Prelims meant to their lives. It would give them the passport to enter the next stage of exam; would drastically cut down their competition from tens of thousands to just under 5000 aspirants; would take them closer to their dreams, goals and liberation. Rao had started writing something. Once done, he turned around, moved a little aside and pointed his index figure at the board. All the eyes turned to the board. In big, blue, bold writing, it read: *"Do the best, leave the rest"*. Most of the candidates were puzzled. Satish too was wondering what Rao wanted to convey. The subsequent Sunday was the Exam and all of them had expected something really inspiring from their mentor. Rao was staring at Satish. Getting on to the centre of the platform, "Friends, I had expected to see you all brim with confidence... you all had toiled day in and day out for the past many months and years, you have stayed away from your close friends, parents, relatives...everyone and... have given your full commitment to realise your dreams. But I am disappointed to say, I can only see fear in most of your eyes. This really troubles me... I am puzzled. When I had given my 100 per cent and you had put in your 100 per cent, what is the reason to fear? I am clueless." He paused for a minute and continued, "...Do not turn me into a Mahavishnu by turning yourselves into Arjun. You are fully ready for the Exam this moment and for some strange reasons you too fear the very war you have been preparing for. This Exam presents you with many uncertainties, I am fully aware of that. The apparently brightest student here might not even clear that Prelims and the last person in the queue might come out at the top of the list. It happens every year, year after year..." Satish was engrossed in the talk, like most others. Rao, after taking a quick look at wall clock, continued, "What matters is how far you are willing to go...not where you have come from. According to me, the only thing that counts beyond this point is not your IQ or gold medals...it is only your grit. Be bold", he further added, "Do not lose heart when you come across questions from unknown areas...Or when you are not able to attend questions even from your strong areas. Do not feel let down by the question paper...there are always certain shocks and surprises every year and that holds true for everyone taking the exam – including the toppers. Never let those things bog you down. Just be relaxed. Give your best shot. Leave the rest."

Amidst the chaos and clutter around, Satish could still hear those words reverberating inside him. Selvi gave the usual pet knock on his head. Satish smiled and resumed sipping his fresh lime soda. "Okay…bye!" Both of them parted ways from the Famous Fruit Juice.

It seemed like the longest night yet in Satish's life. 13.05.2000. The merciless Delhi summer too played its part. Satish was lying on his cot, struggling to sleep. He closed his eyes tightly. In about twelve hours he would be holding the Prelims GS question paper in his hands. Those 150 questions will significantly decide if he would appear in the Mains exam or not; whether he would realise his secret and impossible dream of becoming an IAS officer or not. Myriad statistics and key points across the areas like world climatic regions, sports events, theories of learning, budget deficits, consciousness cylce and the like constantly made unwanted, guest appearances in his mind. The memories of Madurai Collectorate came and went, frequently. The tragedy of Mohit and the cyclones too flashed in his mind. He tried to calm down. "You need to have sound sleep on the night prior to the exam"*:* right from chotu to Rao everyone had advised him that. Satish was more than willing to sleep; but sleep did not like him that night. The small alarm clock was fully prepared to wake him up at 6:00AM. He had marked a dozen topics to be revised on the morning of the Exam. He had planned to complete the revision before leaving at eight. He had realised during AIC's model tests that revisions hold the key to scoring well. Without a couple of revisions he felt things just vanished from his mind. It was half past eleven.

A frustrated Satish got up from the cot and reached out for a cigarette. He could hear Hardeep snoring. Satish stood by the window and took quick, restless puffs. "Why am I tense?...anyway I have Maharaja Wines for me. This IAS-thing was just a one-year deal.. how can I become IAS? ..why should I be a collector? ..I took five years even to complete my BE…" His eyes were strained and he wanted to sleep badly. He hit the bed after three Milds. 1:00 AM. "Am I really appearing in the IAS Exams?!" At a distance, he could hear the dogs quarrelling for their territories.

Satish was on the verge of going mad. He gave up the efforts to sleep and got up from the cot. 1:30 AM. Got out of his room and reached down. He went to the park across the road and started walking briskly. "Don't worry *saar*.. the taxi will be here at 8:00AM sharp. Sunday morning… you will be at the exam centre even before 9!",

Senthil, the Tamil tiffin*wala* had promised him in the evening. The topics reserved for revision in the morning chased him liked a ghost. "...I should at least clear the Prelims...even that is enough to make him ecstatic." The mere thought of letting his father down, strangely, sent a chill down his spine. "R.Satish I.A.S...sounds good", with a cigarette between his lips Satish was staring at the dusty hot sky. He remembered Kumar telling him about the recent blockbuster *Muthalvan* where the hero gets a chance to be the state Chief Minister for a day. For a moment he imagined himself to be the Madurai District Collector for a day. "I will set right the health-related issues in the first hour. The whole system of GH-PHC is rotten. The government hospitals look like our bus stands..people all over but no one to take care. Chaos, noise and stench. Even Maharaja bar was much better than these hospitals. I will change all the non-performing doctors, officers, nurses and staff, get in the best team, pass orders to construct a brand new hospital for the district...all GHs should be like Apollo Hospitals.." Satish finished his plan for the twenty fourth hour with the arrest of a local criminal-MLA.

He could see the first ray of light of the day. 5:30AM. 14.05.2000. Prelims day. With dead and wide open eyes Satish was planning to leave the park. This first-time experience of insomnia had numbed his senses. He could barely hear the early birds that were chirping from the huge trees in the park. Some frail, old men and women had already reached the park with their walking sticks. Satish was frustrated. Cursing his father for his wild ambition of making his truant son a District Collector, Satish started walking back to his room. Tea shops and temples were already full of people. Satish had two *matri* and a special tea before finally reaching his room. The thermacol above his desk had a paper slip with the list of topics to be revised. He picked up the science and technology class room notes and quickly turned a few pages. "*Beep..beep... Beep..beep...*", the time piece had touched 6:00AM. Satish pressed it reflexively and silenced it. S&T was followed by the wildlife sanctuaries in India.

It was not the time piece alarm now. "*Ding ..dong*", the door bell. Satish was jerked. Irritated. "Which bastard comes at this hour..." He left the pages flap in the fan wind and went for the flat door. By then the tube light in Hardeep's room was on. Satish opened the door. Satish could not believe his own tired eyes. He took a few seconds to recognise the persons standing in front of him. "What?!!", he tried to utter. His tired eyes were filled with tears now. His father and Kumar were full of joy to be there.

A few minutes past 12 noon. The optional subject paper had started at 10:00AM; it was for 2 hours. Hundreds of candidates started pouring out of the academic buildings of Kendriya Vidyala, with hope and despair; with confidence and shattered dreams; with relief and trauma. Rajaraman and Kumar were trying to locate Satish in the sea of candidates. They were both thrilled even to be waiting outside the Exam centre. "I hope he has done well", Rajaraman said after spotting Satish coming out of the school building. Kumar could not still believe his fellow Desperado had appeared in the IAS exams. Clutching the GS question paper, Satish came towards them. His eyes were burning red. His fingers were trembling.

There was a break of more than 2 hours before the GS paper started at 2:30PM. Dozens of parents, friends, boyfriends, relatives, drivers, well wishers, distant uncles and the like waited with snacks, lunch parcels, juice bottles, and study material for the afternoon's papers. The nearby canteen was also ready to do a brisk business. A few tea vendors on cycles lined up around the campus despite the cruel sun. The crowd of candidates marching out spotted their respective relative and friends. Satish too reached the dark shade of the huge neem tree where the father-friend duo was waiting for him.

The excited Rajaraman hugged his son, "Hope you have done well." Kumar snatched the booklet of questions from Satish's hand, "Let me have a look!!" His curiosity to have a look at the IAS question paper was beyond control. Rajaraman made his son sit comfortably on the broken platform around the neem tree. Kumar looked at Satish and gave a reassuring smile. There were a dozen other candidates and their support teams taking refugee under the tree. The merciless sun was blazing. The tree also did not want to pick up a fight with the sun. It just gave in to the heat. "Do not ask me anything mummy ...all my efforts have gone waste. I will never become an IAS officer" a just-out-of-college girl was venting her frustration on her mother. The mother's consoling words did not reach her ears. She kept pushing her mother before finally breaking down inconsolably. Kumar had a quick look at this drama that unfolded right next to them before resuming with the question paper booklet. "I have got 83 correct", "What is the answer for this question...", "I have so much to revise for the afternoon", "One more attempt!", "The cutoff will be only 59 this time", "No, No! Check out the last model paper in CSR": some random murmurs that fell on Rajaraman's ears. He could not arrive at any conclusion from them.

Satish did not have any specific expression on his face. He did not utter a single word. The hot wind blowing around seemed to be directed at his face. The intensity seemed to get stronger. His head and heart were getting hotter. The image of the imposing school building gradually blurred in front of him. The discrete murmurs around grew louder and louder. He felt his father and Kumar were standing next to him and holding him, probably supporting him and preventing him from losing balance; but he was not sure. His vision got further diminished. He felt he was falling asleep. Or was he dying? The voices turned into loud, low-pitched noises. His eyes closed completed. He collapsed.

The father-friend team was horrified. Satish had collapsed under the neem tree. Rajaraman could not bear the sight. Kumar was scared to the hilt. Trying to maintain his calm Kumar grabbed the water bottle from the bag and sprinkled generously on his best friend's face. By then a couple of others too had joined his efforts. One elderly man tried to ease out the situation by asking everyone to get back. "Make him lie on the platform… unbutton his shirt…let him get some space…do not crowd, please." Rajaraman was shell-shocked.

A few minutes later Satish's swollen eyes opened for a while before gradually closing again. The crowd around had a momentary relief in the meantime. Kumar came running with a pack of glucose and a bottle of juice in his hand. "There is a hospital nearby." someone said. Kumar took Satish in his arms, wiped the off water from his face and tried to make Satish's head rest on his shoulder. He gestured to the old man nearby to mix some glucose in the fruit juice. They tried to make Satish take in a few sips. Satish slowly did.

Only one more hour was left for the afternoon optional papers. The crowd around had thinned. "This is enough...get an auto." Rajaraman shocked and helpless told Kumar. Kumar too felt like doing so. He tried to softly place Satish on the platform. But Satish did not allow to be placed down. He shook his head feebly. Rajaraman came near him and patted him on his cheek. Satish tried hard to open his eyes. Gradually, he could. Kumar offered him some more glucose-juice. This time Satish was able to lift his hand and hold the bottle.

Rajaraman felt relieved.

Thousands of rats. Lakhs of people. Utter noise. Unimaginable chaos. Non stop bustle. Mountains of luggage. Porters in red uniform. Long trains carrying thousands of people away from the city and into it every hour. The red LED bulbs of the digital clock in platform number 12 of the New Delhi railway station showed 22:22 PM. "Once again you have turned a hero! Had some media people been there they would have flashed the news…a true gladiator amidst the candidates! Hats off to your will-power." Hardeep told Satish. The Prelims drama at KV had reach everyone in Old Rajinder Nagar. Kumar too joined, "Of course…even I find it unbelievable …also very proud... can't believe this bugger actually had so much in him. He collapsed like a dead man…and got up like a …he-man. This is really too much for me to handle…I still can't believe that this rowdy had actually appeared in the IAS exam…and now this comeback drama at the exam centre… something out-of-the-world!"

For the kind attention of the passengers. Train number 2622, New Delhi-Chennai Tamil Nadu Express is ready to leave from platform number 12. Three "ding" tones followed the digital announcement.

Rajaraman was just awed by the sheer grit his son had shown the previous day. In fact, unable to bear his son's plight that afternoon, even he had given up. He wanted to rush his son to the nearest hospital, away from the exam centre. He wanted to call off the whole Maharaja-IAS deal and take his son back from Delhi forever. "To hell with IAS!" He felt his utterly foolish, wild dream was the root of his son's sufferings. But the way Satish fought back and proceeded to appear in the post-lunch optional paper simply electrified him. Rao's feedback about Satish also had taken Rajaraman close to nirvana. "Your son will definitely become an IAS officer." Those words of Rao would never fade from the proud father's memory. Rajaraman could also not come to terms with the fact that this very same kid had been a constant pain for everyone around. This transformation was something Rajaraman had read only in stories.

The red signal turned yellow. The electric engine cried loudly. A beaming Rajaraman shook hands with Hardeep and got in the A1 coach of the TN Express. Kumar and Satish hugged Hardeep before punching his tummy and getting into the moving train. "See you soon." Satish shouted while waving at his preparation roommate.

TN Express picked speed. New Delhi railway station faded away.

PART VII: BIRDS RETURN

The migratory birds of Old Rajinder Nagar went to their respective homes after appearing in the Prelims and returned to Delhi in the first week of June. Usually the coaching classes for the Mains started in the first week of June. These classes were mainly for the second optional paper, though some classes were taken for the GS papers too. The Mains started in the second half of October. Unlike Prelims where the candidates were given just two, two-hour objective papers, the Mains continued for days together like *Dussehra* and the papers were of descriptive type. The marks taken in Mains, along with the interview marks, went into deciding one's position in the final rank list. Out of over one lakh candidates who appeared in the Prelims, around 5000 were selected for the Mains. The Prelims result was usually out in the first half of August. It was like this: June – Mains classes. August – Prelims result. October – Mains.

"Forget my story…do you really think you can contribute better by being in a government service.. you could probably have contributed more by doing some research or working abroad and remitting money…or…could have…", Satish was promptly interrupted by Hardeep: "Why do you have this doubt?"

"Bhaiya…masala chai?", the mobile chai vendor offered. Hardeep and Satish got a cup each. Satish took out a Milds. They enjoyed sitting on the lawn. It was the second week of June. Satish was back in Delhi after a short break in Madurai for about a fortnight. He returned to Delhi with loads of yummy Madurai snacks and some new clothes. The Mains classes for the optional papers had started in the preceding week. On Rao's advice Satish ended up taking Geography as his second optional. The classes were picking up. It being a Sunday evening Harry and Sat had come out for a short break. Shining soap bubbles. Stuffed giant elephant toys. Couples sitting close to each other beyond the reach of the lights. Obese men running behind their two feet tall kids. Light emitting mini-parachutes landing on the dark lawns. Bunch of teenagers commenting on the girls and

aunties passing by. Impeccably dressed men from the defence services. Very active *bhelpuriwalas*. Some transgenders continuing with their harassment. Naked kids jumping into the duck ponds nearby. Photographers promising a world-class print in under 10 minutes. Amidst all this was standing the well-lit, inspiring structure – India Gate. It was just under 30 minutes from Old Rajinder Nagar.

"What do you mean…everyone has this doubt! Can someone really change the system? It is a waste of time. We have all heard stories about punishment postings, transfers, vigilance, suspensions…of upright officers. It gets frustrating beyond a point…"

Hardeep interrupted his flat-mate again: "Boss, I don't claim to bring about some revolution in bureaucracy…but…well, let me try and explain it to you this way… listen..One day I was walking down a beach which was littered with thousands of starfishes which had been washed ashore. It was still early morning and as sun would come up, these starfishes would soon die in the scorching heat. Well, that's how the nature works. The beach was largely deserted. However my eyes caught a small boy who was merrily jumping along the shore picking up one starfish after another and throwing it into sea. I was puzzled. I walked up to the boy and asked him – What are you doing?" Hardeep took a sip before continuing. Satish was engrossed, he took a long, strong puff. "…He answered while continuing to throw the starfishes back to sea – so that they at least survive rather than die on the shore. I was amused. Trying to hide my smile I told him – This is going to take you years. Look *chotu*, there are thousands of starfish littered all over; Even if you do it the whole day you can save only a few dozens. It is a waste of time…do you feel it can make a difference? The boy turned around and said – Well you ask me will it make a difference… And he added as he picked one more starfish and threw into sea – it did make a difference to this starfish…is it not?"

Satish was silent for a few seconds and broke it with, "Ooooh!! My friend Socrates!! You have opened my eyes!! I will go to Marina beach rightaway… and start picki." Hardeep's kick ensured that Satish did not complete the word and the sentence. "Okay relax Mr.Starfish.. er..Mr.Socrates", Satish was laughing aloud and rolling on the lawns.

But for those occasional showers no one could make out it was monsoon. Only winters and summers were harsh there. The teacher-lecturer was busy explaining Koppen's climatic classification of the world to the jam-packed class. The white board was full of sketches of the world map and a few tabulations in red and blue. Satish was perched in one of the corner seats in the last row. Here again, just like it was during the Prelims classes, Satish could not categorise the candidates as anything other than "IAS aspirants". Some were fresh. A few others were more than a quarter century old, landing up in the coaching class lecture hall after completing post graduation and working somewhere for sometime for some reasons. A few others were on the verge of completing three decades of life on this planet. Some had planned to appear in the Exams almost a year later, in May 2001. Some others were listening to the same story of Koppen for the second time, planning to try their luck at the Exams for the fourth time the subsequent year. Some of them were there after doing some research and acquiring PhD degrees. Some were from distant districts like Dimapur, some were from Colaba. Some students took down notes in long registers, others in loose sheets of A4 papers to be filed at the end of the day. Some were just quietly chatting with the nearby girl or the boy. Some wore Puma, others Paragon. Some wanted to serve the country by giving everything to clear the Exam. Some others had ideas to cash on the "civil servant" tag during their weddings. A few others were interested in using the Exam for world tours. Some relished the power and status they would be given once they cleared the Exam. Some of them were passionate about wearing the khaki uniform. Some were there to promote their love life. Instant fame was the driving force for some others. Some had IAS in their hearts and minds right from school days. Some were the sons and daughters of serving bureaucrats. Many had T.N.Seshan or Kiran Bedi as their role models. Some others came there to enjoy city life in the fullest sense; they found the tag "IAS aspirant" fancier than "unemployed youth".

"Mains is a different ball-game. Writing answers has to be practised regularly, sincerely. Also for geography keep practising sketches and outlines of world map, map of India and important diagrams under each topic. Time is a luxury which you people don't have… start now!" the lecturer wrapped up the class with a thump on the Godrej desk. The crowd of aspirants including Satish made a hurried beeline for Tinku's special *chai.*

July 2000. "He is reaching tomorrow!" an excited Selvi told Satish. Satish had been dying to hear this good news ever since the day Mohit left for his cyclone devastated state. There was no word from him after that. During these many months that passed by Satish had spent many days consoling Selvi. Rao's repeated attempts to contact Mohit had also been fruitless. Though the Exam preparation consumed their days and nights, the loveable Mohit was in the back of everyone's mind. "But why did he not even call you for so long?", Satish's anger tried to engulf his joy. "He is like that", Selvi was too happy to say anything else. The horror of the cyclone flashed in Satish's mind. He wanted to forget those haunting memories, but they would not go away. "Okay I will meet both of you after the class tomorrow", Satish said.

No sooner than the geography lecturer finished his session on hill area development, Satish waded through the crowd frantically and came down the stairs jumping to reach the main road. He looked at the other side to look for his good, old friend and Selvi. They were not near Tinku's. Speedily scanning the area around the tea shop Satish crossed the road without caring for the rickshaws, scooters and wild cars. "Probably they are at the book stall." Satish had crossed the road. He walked toward the book stall. "There!!" Satish ran towards him and jumped and hugged Mohit, "You useless bugger!!" Mohit was moved to see Satish.

After leaving Delhi for Orissa, it had taken Mohit a few days to even reach his village. What was in store for him there was a personal catastrophe. The cyclone had wiped out his entire village. Not even a single human being was left untouched. Goats, cows and even the huge trees were not spared. It had taken Mohit almost ten months to recover from the trauma. Satish felt a chill down his spine when he heard the turns Mohit's life had taken after he left them. "And…my IAS dreams...they too were destroyed by the cyclone…I was not able to appear in the Prelims…I have crossed the age limit now. I wanted to develop my village as a model village…I wanted to show case it to the whole world…Rao sir too wanted that…My parents wanted that…Now…", Satish and Selvi were too disturbed to console Mohit. Satish remembered those days when he roamed aimlessly in the streets of Old Rajinder Nagar and how the affable Mohit had tried to help him out; Satish also believed that there was something called as fate. "Else there was no reason for this sincere chap to be out of the IAS race…and where was this destiny taking me…the most unfit person for this race. I hope somehow Mohit gets to appear in the Exam...impossible."

Satish tried to start, "... try to...there are opportunities Mohit…you will surely.." That was when the commotion from Tinku's interrupted the three.

They turned to see a terrified group of aspirants standing around the tea shop and witnessing something. People from the nearby shops were also running to be a part of the crowd. The stray dogs scattered. The monkeys watched from the roof tops. Satish and Mohit took quick steps and tried to break in the crowd. Selvi too attempted to follow them. Satish somehow managed to push a few of them and got closer to the scene. Mohit went closely behind him. For a moment they could not absorb fully what was happening. Their eyes saw and ears heard, but the brains refused to accept. Their hearts seemed to shatter and tear their bodies apart. A hefty man in his forties was thrashing Tinku with the tea pan. The gas stove was still burning. Half-made tea was spilt all over the place. Tinku was not yelling – he was beyond that; he was lying like a small piece of log, motionless. Everyone around was numb; no one said or did anything. At times Tinku desperately tried and managed to lift his hand; but the tea pan came down heavily. Repeatedly. Selvi could not still break in the crowd, she did not have any idea what was going on there. It was good for her. The *rickshawalas* on the road had stopped to catch a glimpse of what was happening. The traffic had come to a halt. Mohit's face turned red and eyes moist. The place got noisier.

The man, who was almost on the verge of killing Tinku, mouthed a few more expletives before lifting the sauce pan for another heavy landing. That was when, jumping out of nowhere, Satish picked up the burning stove with all his strength. Within a moment the man gave out a nasty yell and was lying on the floor next to Tinku in a pool of blood – his own blood. His skull had almost been spilt from the back. Almost. The stove got fully covered with its own rapid fire, as it landed beside the man. Mohit was stunned; his mouth was wide open. That was the case with most people in the crowd. Some of them even turned the other side unable to bear the sight of blood freely flowing out of the cracked head. Satish picked up the sauce pan, and like someone possessed by an evil spirit, started thrashing the man. The burning stove had turned into a huge ball of fire. The crowd yelled. Some moved away. Some of them felt giddy and groped for the shoulders of those nearby. Selvi had no clue about this. She was still in the outer circle. Mohit batted his eyelids. Somehow he mustered courage to go near Satish and tried to restrain him. But Satish did not seem to stop; he seemed to have decided to kill him.

Suddenly, the chaos appeared to peak. Almost the entire crowd started to disperse in all directions. The fire ball had grown bigger. Two police constables came running towards Satish. Within moments the entire crowd had vanished. The long *lathi* of one of cops landed sharply on Satish's back bone. "Bastard!" Satish closed his eyes tightly, held his back and fell on the floor. His white T-shirt turned red quickly.

It was not a busy day for the Old Rajinder Nagar police station across Shankar Road. Only two FIRs till then. The SHO of Old Rajinder Nagar police station had a huge, untidy desk in front of him. Across the desk Mohit and Rao were sitting on those S-shaped rusty, steel chairs. Satish was standing beside the SHO. "This is the problem with today's youth sir*ji*..", the SHO pompously continued, "..they think they can create a revolution.. they take law in their own hands.. they want to be like the film heroes.." Rao and Mohit nodded emphatically; they did not have any other choice. The cop continued while tapping his *lathi* on Satish's shoulder, "Look at this bastard… he has come from Madras… for becoming an officer...but he does not want to study…he wants to be the local don…*goonda.* The problem sir*ji* is with his parents… sons rich parents are like this only…they want to be their own bosses…they do not want to follow any rules.. Sir*ji*..let me ask you one thing.. if everyone takes law in his hands what will happen to this country? What for are we wearing this uniform and working day and night without rest ..." The SHO continued without any break, without expecting a reply from anyone. "We should correct such criminals at the earliest stage itself...else..." Satish did not hear most of the remaining part. His heart was with Tinku, who had been admitted to the Gangaram Hospital. Lifting the *lathi* from Satish's shoulder, "What would have happened had the man died... how could you have got your student out...that too like this without any FIR? You should think about such things." Rao kept quiet. "This time I leave this scoundrel... but sir*ji* you will not have someone to help you always...", Rao nodded respectfully. "...and don't think I am leaving him just because of the DC *saab*...I usually give such people one chance. Next time this happens.." For a moment Rao missed track of how the SHO's statement ended. He remembered and felt immensely grateful for his former student who had been recently posted as the Additional DCP, Central District, Delhi Police.

Satish too felt like meeting and thanking the officer.

It was August 1, 2000. Satish was excitedly opening the courier from his father. It was a beautiful olive green greeting card with "Best of luck" embossed on it in golden letters. Innumerable feeble outlines of tiny pink roses could be seen all over the olive backdrop. "My dear

Satish... best of luck for the results. I am already proud to be your father. Love, father". A small paper packet of *prasadam* from the Meenakshi temple accompanied the card.

Satish could manage only the last row again. It was a class on sustainable agriculture. The lecturer had asked them to pay good attention to the topic as it was a hot area for the question-setters. The lecturer started with the pre-Independence agriculture growth rates, the food crisis and emergence of green revolution and came to the topic within a few minutes. Satish tried to focus on the class; but painfully realised he was unable to do so. His mind wandered out of the class, out of the syllabus. "Will I clear the Prelims?" "One of the key components of sustainable agriculture is integrated nutrient management" "Do I deserve to write Mains?" "..ICAR in collaboration with" "I think I have given my best". "Crop diversity is the need of..." "Roll number 141182... adds up to eight. My lucky number". "extensive mechanisation is not necessarily a bane" "Already proud? Nonsense. Focus. Focus". "Nature provides for everyone's need, not for greed" "What if I clear?!" Satish's face developed a grin by itself that he tried to hide. "Okay students...practise well. Don't waste time... and very good luck for the results!" Satish managed to wake up his neighbour before getting out of the lecture room.

It seemed every electron in Old Rajinder Nagar was excited. "Yes confirmed news...its going to be out anytime today!" 16 August 2000. Already dozens of candidates had flocked the UPSC building, Dholpur House. The desk clerk at the UPSC was having a testing time attending to the hundreds of non-stop phone calls from across the country. "Probably by today or tomorrow...latest by next week it is planned. Yes, yes. . . Okay"; he put down the handset after reciting that before picking up the ringing phone once again to repeat the same, in the same tone. For the ordinary ears his reply did not seem to divulge any tangible information. But for the desperate hundreds who called, even that was a concrete reply. Somehow they were very sure the results were to be out on that very day. Selvi had been to the Hanuman temple on a special visit. Mohit too had accompanied her. For the numerous thousands who had taken the Prelims, positive results meant their competition is drastically cut short and they have moved closer to their goals and dreams. Negative results meant either they were totally out of the field or would have to continue with their prison-like preparation life for one more year till the 2001 Prelims. Hardeep had stayed overnight at his friend's room in the same locality. He had gone there to catch up with a few of his old pals. Rao was sincerely praying that all his deserving students would clear the Prelims.

Satish had called Rajaraman that morning. It was his mother's birth anniversary. "God bless you. Okay. . . let me know about the results soon. I am hoping for the best...but in any case you are welcome back home anytime Satish...you have already proved yourself... you should not worry about anything or get disappointed. Our one-year pact is about to be over...and you are already a winner in my eyes. In fact I plan to give you Maharaja the very day you reach Madurai.. I am very proud of you...God bless you." a hyper Rajaraman had told Satish. Satish was trying to do some writing practice before going for the afternoon geography class. He was trying hard, but he could not. It seemed the whole world worked against him and stopped him from doing anything specific. He tried to focus, he could not. The chaotic waves of Exam-IAS-preparation-father-results-Rao-cyclone-Collector, constantly lapped the shores of his mind. The waves were vigorous too. Satish took deep puffs of 555. He had ditched Milds. It was the fourth one for the day. He pitied himself. He was not very sure what he was expecting from the results; worse, he was not even sure what he was supposed to expect from the results. "I really wonder how thousands of candidates are able to go through this unexplainable torture year after year, attempt after attempt!" stubbing the cigarette he got off the chair and reached for the window. "I am sure Harry will pass. He is from IIT." The members of a few monkey families were jumping from one roof top to the other, one after the other. The last one to jump was an over-weight mother with her baby clinging to her. Satish smiled. For a moment he remembered Rao's class on Harlow. He remembered his mother.

He remembered his father. *Raddiwala's* rhythm made Satish look down the lane. "Good business!" Satish told himself on noticing the three gunny bags tied to the *raddiwala's* bicycle; they were absolutely full. A mal-nourished dog followed the bicycle. Tens of pigeons were adding beauty to the otherwise dead sky.

Satish went back to the desk and lit another 555 before reaching for the window again. "At last the door is open! Wow!!...what a girl!" Satish exclaimed on fixing his eyes on the girl in the opposite balcony. He quickly moved a little back in an attempt to be away from the girl's sight and continued to see her. The girl was busy looking down the street as if she was in charge of collecting toll from everyone who walked the street. She was wearing a sleeveless bright top and dark pyjamas. The bright top was not very tight. "How can someone be so attractive!! Sexy body." Satish desperately wished to be on that balcony; wished to be standing beside her; wished to have his hand on her delicate shoulder; wished she turned towards him; wished she came near him; wished he could hug her; wished he could feel her body; wished.. "No no.. I wish she were here next to me in this room. No.. I wish I was with her inside her room. I wish she too wanted to.." *Bang-Bang-Bang!!*, those heavy thuds on his doors mercilessly shattered his world and brought him back to his own room. "Who the hell is that ass?" He moved towards the door cursing the person at the door for spoiling his fantasy.

Hardeep was anxious, as expected. It was his second attempt and already his college batch mates, who had taken jobs in the campus placements, had accumulated handsome bank balances. Many others who preferred higher studies had completed one year of their MS course in some top ranked US Universities. Those who had decided to be at the IIMs had done their summer placements and were looking forward to the day-zero placements and six-digit packages. Here, he was spending his second year at his cellular room in Old Rajinder Nagar, shelling out huge amounts as coaching class fees, room rent, *tiffinwala* bill, *chaiwala* account, PCO bills etc; and trying to master subjects as eclectic as ancient Indian history and I.C. engines and theories of human emotions, with his identity as "IAS aspirant". He badly wanted to be selected that year, at least in his second attempt. Unable to be at ease in his room, he decided to catch up with his old friends and be more relaxed at the time of the results. They had finished a few bottles of beer the previous night. By the next morning they were sure that results were to be declared any moment that day. It was around 1PM when they were about to have some food, the UPSC decided to make the results of Prelims 2000 public. Without any advance notice or any sort of feelers, as abruptly as it could get, the list of the candidates who were eligible for the Mains was neatly put up in the special notice boards kept in the UPSC campus. The news spread faster than a wildfire. A collage of disappointment and joy was being made. Hardeep and friends had taken an auto rickshaw to the Dholpur House. Hardeep was sure at the bottom of his heart that he would clear the Prelims; he wished to get selected for IPS in the final list. He was relieved to see the notice board. He had cleared. Then he restlessly searched for the roll number 141182.

Bang-Bang-Bang!!, Hardeep almost broke open the door and pounced on Satish while screaming, "You have cleared bastard!!"

PART VIII: MAIN COURSE

The rush in front of Maharaja Wines did not seem to be the normal one. For 1030 AM, a crowd of close to twenty people was something unusual. The evening crowd at the Maharaja bar was expected to touch a century, easily. The Prelims result that had been announced two weeks back had reached almost everyone, to be precise everyone who drank, in Madurai. Maharaja Wines was the talk of the town. Though he tried hard, it was beyond the means of Rajaraman to manage his excitement. Among many other things, he also ensured that a board was put up in front of Maharaja for one whole month: "5% off on every bottle" Probably it was the first time in the history of liquor shops in Madurai, probably in the whole country, that someone had offered discount on liquor – that too for one full month. It was the third week of the liquor discount *mela* at Maharaja. The crowd had obviously multiplied over the days. "Congrats!! Hearty wishes!!" Most of the regular buyers complimented Rajaraman before going away with some bottles. "I heard your son has become Collector", an old man heartily laughed and wished Rajaraman before opening the bottle-cap and moving away. "Unbelievable! He was a rogue…it is all destiny. Star positions…nothing is in our hands.. very happy!", an old friend of Rajaraman said over the phone. In fact, just like anyone else, even Rajaraman could not digest the truth. When Satish had called him to convey the result, Rajaraman, in sheer disbelief, had asked Satish to check out the results once again, properly. Rajaraman had also given Satish's roll number to some of his friends to verify if what Satish had told him was actually true or was he just dreaming. But all the repeated, independent checks just confirmed what Hardeep had seen in the UPSC notice board – Satish had cleared Prelims. He was one among the 5000 or so candidates who were lucky and competent enough to take the Mains. Rajaraman thanked everyone with a Colgate smile while accepting cash and putting it in the fast-filling cash box. The shop boys had a tough day managing the super crowd. Maharaja Wines looked like the opening show of a new Rajni movie. *Kalyani 13. McDowels half 8. 11 Honeybee full.* People were shouting out their orders trying hard to get the attention of the shop boys who wished they had many more hands. The bottles were flying off the shelves and the crates were flying off the shop. Rajaraman too wished he had more hands to handle cash. His right hand even started to pain. The cash box was emptied to a suitcase twice. Dozens of hands were trying hard to make him accept cash and give them their share. “Calm down. One at a time…we have enough stock for the day”, Rajaraman tried pacifying them while picking up further speed. Occasionally even he irritatingly ordered the shop boys to work faster. Interestingly, amidst the hands holding the currency notes one of the hands stood out – it had a brown envelope instead of the usual currency note.

Rajaraman did not notice it first. But prompted by some strange intuition he reached out for the envelope and grabbed it. He took a quick glance at what it was and excitedly got up from his seat. The envelope had his son’s name and his Delhi address on it. It had come from the UPSC. Rajaraman tried to locate the person who had handed out the envelope. He was pleasantly shocked to see Satish on the other side of the counter. “Is it really him? Am I dreaming? No…he is actually here.”

Satish, Kumar, Rajaraman and one more person were at the dining table in *Satish Villa*. Satish had the envelope and a form in his hand. For those candidates who had cleared Prelims, the UPSC had sent the form for the Mains. One needed to fill in routine details like name, address, educational background, optional subjects chosen for the Mains, exam centre etc. There was also space for achievements, hobbies etc. In addition to all those one also needed to give in his or her service preferences i.e. the preference number for IAS, IPS, IFS and some fifteen or so other services. The list of the services was provided in two columns with a tiny box accompanying each service name. One needed to mark numbers denoting the order of preference corresponding to the services in these boxes. The final allotment of the service was based on this preference list given in the Mains form and the rank one got in the final selection list.

"It is for you to decide.. but you should just mark one against IAS and leave everything else blank..what is the need to fill everything?" Rajaraman was telling Satish. "That is not advisable uncle…if he gives the option for all the services he at least has the chance to get some other service…even if he does not get a high rank to get selected for IAS." Kumar said looking at Satish. "But I don't want him to be anything other than an IAS officer…what is the need? He should become only a District Collector…even the SP works under the Collector." Satish was deep in thought. He tried to listen. "The whole deal was to make him an IAS officer…so why to fill other things?" "That is right uncle, but why to miss the other opportunities…all the selections are for high posts only...audit officer…railway officer...income tax officer.." "Only Collector!", Rajaraman said emphatically looking at the Mains form. He was in no mood to listen to anyone. Satish smiled when he heard Rajaraman say that. He seemed to be thinking of his school and college days.

The fourth person opened the mouth for the first time. "Sir...your son should fill up all the service options...he will do really well in any service. He is very determined...talented! All are very top level posts...you should not leave anything blank. It will not be right. It is like disrespecting the other posts. I have also consulted a few officers I know...like Tirunelveli Corporation Commissioner Mr.Meena...he is a very good friend of mine since his training period in Madurai. He said it was a blunder to leave any option blank. In fact Satish can do very well as an income tax Commissioner also...even railways will be benefited by him. He has the caliber." Kumar and Satish looked at each other and exchanged comments while this person continued with his lecture. It was getting too much for the friends to handle. "Satish... you fill up all the services. Give IAS number one, IPS number two,..I think you can give income tax number three, railways number four...IFS is also very good... you get the chance to visit many foreign countries. Long back there was one...Mr.Chandran as our ambassador to America...he was an able IFS officer", the person went on. Rajaraman was listening to him with due respect. Satish and Kumar seemed to enjoy themselves. "So...start filling like this..." the person completed his lecture.

He was Mr.Sakthivel, the director-owner of EC Engineering College, Madurai.

Satish was at berth number 48 of AS-2 coach of the TN Express speeding towards New Delhi. It was August 24, 2000. He had less than two months to gear himself up for the Mains. He wished that Selvi and Hardeep also got selected in the final list this time. "Even clearing Prelims is a great achievement for me. I should not be greedy. But how did this happen?!" The filled up Mains form was in his bag; the form had just only one service option selected; all other service preferences were crossed out. Only in the box next to 'IAS' Satish had written "1".

"You don't seem to be working enough. This essay will fetch you only fifty to fifty five marks…you need to score at least ninety marks in the essay paper. Look at this…you have written fifteen pages on India's foreign policy without even mentioning a single word on NAM...and without Clinton's visit!", Rao continued as he commented on Satish's answer sheet for the model essay test AIC had conducted for the candidates selected for the Mains, "Your language is not bad…okay, just average…that is enough, but you have to cover all the important points and present them in a good manner. Think well. Its highly competitive and every single mark you score matters a lot...a lot." It was 5th September, 2000. The geography Mains classes were almost over. The final sessions on map work and a few important topics in paper-I were being handled. It was less than forty days for the Mains. The selected candidates had the feeling of being inside a microwave oven; with no one around to switch it off or pull them out. They would continue to have such feeling till the end of the Exam. Satish did not call his father often. He did not have time for that. The white thermacol board near his desk did not have any more space. It was full of bits of papers with points for quick revision across the subjects pinned on it. There was also a tiny magazine clipping with the photo of Mr.Maheshwari, the IAS topper of the year.

Hardeep had shortened his post-lunch song sessions. But for the rare bottle of beer with Satish he did not get up from his chair. For most part of the day Selvi was lost in the assorted columns of books on her desk. She consumed reams of A4 sheet for the answer writing practice. Only in the evenings she came out for *chai* with Mohit. Occasionally they went to Ulan Bator for chicken soup and Agrawal Sweets for quick *rasmalais*. Rao was getting restless with every passing day, as if he was about to appear in the Exams himself. He expected to break his own record results that year. Tinku had recovered almost fully. But he had gone to Bihar. He was to be back only after Diwali.

September 13. The Mains were exactly only one month away from the selected candidates. The seven papers of the Mains totalled 2000 marks. There were two papers each for the compulsory general studies (GS) and the two optional subjects. These six papers were of 300 marks each. There was an essay paper for 200 marks. "Every single mark matters." Mohit kept telling Satish, who by now was on the verge of collapsing any moment for want of bare minimum sleep. "You know…in my second attempt I missed the final ranks by a mere twenty mark. My interview was also bad.. but.. just twenty marks.. just about three marks more in each Mains paper would have fetched me some rank...just three marks out of 300", Mohit also kept repeating his sad stories to Satish. Hardeep started moving to his friends' room in the area to discuss the mechanical engineering optional papers.

September 30. "What's wrong with you.. why do you sound so low?", Kumar shouted from Madurai through the phone. Satish had called him from the PCO across Shankar Road.

"I don't know."

"I think you are under a lot of pressure these days…come on fool…you have already given your best and the whole city is proud of you! You remember the 5% discount sales?!", Kumar continued, "You won't believe…even the other day my dad was asking me to take you as the role model! Imagine...you as role model! Am I really so pathetic in life?! I could not really believe when he told me that! I have been quite sincere and committed to my lorry business…what more he wants? People actually have a very short memory boss! The same person had ordered me to avoid you sometime back..now!" Kumar exclaimed.

Satish tried to laugh and asked in a feeble voice, "He really said that?!"

"Of course fool! Things have changed… don't you still feel that dumbo? And no matter what will happen to your results – you are already a winner. Have told you this a thousand times! If you are not able to take the pressure…just get back here. We are all waiting for you…"

"No… I'm trying ..but I realise I have caught a tiger's tail…even if I want I cannot leave it."

"What?! What are you trying to say… these days you are talking like an intellectual." Kumar said with a grin.

"Don't joke now… you know I did not want this whole IAS thing…I was a hopeless student…but now I feel I am somewhat closer to…something big…I don't know. But there are many intelligent people around… sometimes I feel I should not have cleared the Prelims. The story would have ended there… in a way…in a positive note. But…" Satish went on.

"Wait wait… I agree you are a dumb ass…but you are not the

dumbest one there. Don't tell me everyone around is very intelligent...", Kumar continued matter-of-factly, "See.. from what I have heard and seen when I was with you in Delhi... I am sure the Exam is like a one-day match... glorious uncertainties. You are already in the 40th over fool...you are doing well. Last ten overs...slog it out!"

"No buddy... this is a bloody five day match. Actually.. a marathon.. no...what is it called..mm.. triathlon..no, probably rugby...well...actually a war... W-A-R."

October 1, 2000. The weather in Delhi was getting somewhat pleasant. However for the aspirants it seemed the microwave oven inside which they were getting cooked was adjusted upwards to the "Deep fry" mode. Satish realised how fast a day was over and the next day began; and how this cycle turned faster with every new day. Everyone seemed to experience and understand the difference between planning and doing. All study plans collapsed under the weight of the Mains that was growing bigger and scarier with every passing day.

All the coaching sessions had come to a halt. All the coaching classes had conducted model tests for their candidates. They had tried to have a final pep-up session for their candidates. They wished all their candidates a great success. They wished that more aspirants joined them in the subsequent year. It seemed as though UPSC had cast an inescapable spell on the entire area of Old Rajinder Nagar. Only for the cats, dogs, pigeons and the monkeys of the area, it was life as usual.

In no time the Mains had come and – almost gone. "Do well bro…every mark matters. Forget what had happened so far, what had happened in the morning session…just go with a fresh mind and give your best." Hardeep advised Satish. They were at Kirori Mal College, Delhi University. It was the last day, last paper of Mains for Satish. Psychology paper-II. Paper-I had got over in the morning and it was lunch break. Hardeep was already through with all his papers; through with the Mains. While compulsory papers like the GS, Essay and language papers got over in the first three days of the schedule, the various optional papers were slotted for different dates. Some of the optional papers were right at the beginning while a few others were at the end. Hardeep wanted to stick around in Delhi till the time Satish completed his Mains. But for Satish's Exams, just like any other candidate who had completed his or her Mains, Hardeep too would have headed back home by then. Usually the candidates left for their homes once the Mains got over and returned to Old Rajinder Nagar only for the interview preparation. The Mains results were announced in the month of March, the subsequent year. "You just write something...do not leave any question unanswered..", Hardeep gave his final piece of *gyan* before waving at Satish, who was entering the academic block. His Exam hall was on the second floor room number 311. He climbed up the stairs. He had three Reynolds black ball pens, a Camlin Nouvel 0.5 micro-tip pencil and the folded admit card in his pocket. He had a Natraj transparent foot-scale in his hand. He was clutching it tightly that. With every step he took, his mind got more and more overwhelmed. "What if I botch up even paper-II...morning was a disaster!! How on earth was I supposed to know the latest Indian studies on attitude formation?! Rascals!" "I hope I don't get anything from research methods." "Anyway... all this seems to be a waste of time...how can I clear?" "Somehow..God...give me one 60-marker from sports psychology...I will crack it!"

Three hours later. A long bell. One of the invigilators announced, thumping the desk, "Okay, stop writing...submit the answer sheets." The other invigilator, a lady, walked briskly down the aisle between the desks on the left half of the Exam hall and started snatching away the answer sheets, from one candidate after the other. "Ma'm.. ma'm..please..please... one minute..", the candidate in the last row was not in a mood to hand over the answer sheet. The invigilator was also in no mood to leave it. She snatched it and came towards Satish. In the meantime the other invigilator had finished collecting the answer sheets from the rows on the right half of the hall. "Thank God!! Its all over!", Satish told himself; he felt a huge load fly off his shoulders and heart. The exhaustion and fatigue that he had accumulated over the past one year – just vanished like magic. "Thanks madam", Satish handed over his psychology paper-II answer sheets to the one, who was on the prowl. "Hmm", the lady invigilator nodded and proceeded to add to her kitty of freshly collected answer sheets. Satish also thanked the One above and the person who set the paper for giving him a big question on sports psychology. He then got up and looked around the hall; but for a few, all others had left the place. The remaining ones were packing their ammunition like water bottles, admit cards, pens, sketch pens etc. Satish proceeded to walk out of the hall. With every passing moment, he felt getting elevated to a newer level of satisfaction and contentment. He did not know how to classify the feeling; nevertheless he liked it. He felt immensely happy about himself. He did not exactly recollect where it – the entire IAS journey – had started, but he was delighted that he had come to the point of completing the Mains. "Sometimes the whole thing feels like a dream!" happily talking to himself he came outside room 311. "Oops!! Sor…", Satish was not in a state of mind to complete his apology as he could not believe his eyes, when he noticed the person with whom he had almost collided. "It's okay", the lady candidate casually said and went past Satish. "What?!!", Satish was flying. His contentment turned into excitement and euphoria.

He was losing grip of Natraj. His heart was melting. He stood there as if stuck by a lightning. He shook his head and tried to come down to earth. He failed. His eyes were constantly fixed on the girl who had by then reached the far end of the corridor. She was in a bright red orange and a pair of faded blue jeans. She was wearing a pair of beautiful black leather slippers. Her jet black ponytail caressed the cotton kurta. And she was as gorgeous as Satish had seen her on the day of the Prelims results – in the balcony opposite.

It was close to midnight. Satish finished counting the cash before bundling it and placing inside the worn out briefcase. It was Rs.65,690 and some change. "Good business brother…Weekends will cross 1 lakh." the store boy said while taking stock. He was also trying to bring some order to a row of unopened Bagpiper bottles in one of the middle racks. "RC fully sold out…it was a mad crowd today." the store boy continued while doing his job. "No.. we can double this sales..", Satish replied casually while locking the briefcase. "Look, even with this primitive bar we are able to sell a lot.. about say, 50 to 60,000 average daily. What if we give a complete image makeover to our bar… we will give the best ambience to drink in the whole Madurai city. College students will surely start crowding in hundreds here..we also got a great location." The store boy listened with an open mind and an open mouth. "The place needs to have ..say…an ultra-modern ambience.. Even a live performance by some local troupe..or something.." The store boy now burst into laughter. "Live show in our bar?! You must be joking bro!" Satish took a few moments and continued with a serious tone, "Hmm… probably it is beyond..hmm... you have been around for many years.. but my ideas will definitely work out here. The crowd will find it entirely new.. probably the only place in south India to do so.." Satish continued, "er..south of Chennai". By then the duo had come out and the shutters were about to be downed. "It will work out." Satish turned towards the road and seemed to be telling himself. That was when the police constable stopped his bicycle in front of Maharaja Wines. "So…how are things? I heard you have cleared IAS exam..mm…", the constable continued with a blatantly sarcastic tone, "you will come here as our Collector?" "No sir..I have given Exam sir.. just here.. er…waiting for results" Satish mumbled. The constable turned his face while looking at the store boy who was busy locking the shutter, "I heard you sell a lot of local stuff… uh?" The boy raised the shutter and came near Satish. "No sir.. my father never does it…that is why Maharaja is." "What?! You mean to say I am lying? You argue with me?...you think you are already the District Collector?", the furious constable interrupted Satish. A few moments of silence. The store boy came held Satish's hand and told the constable, "Sir..business is doing well sir… boss wanted to see you even last night sir… but... today he left early sir... he will come tomorrow sir.." The constable gave a nasty look, "So? Big IAS Collector is standing right here." Satish looked at the store boy. The store boy was looking at the constable. The constable was looking at Satish. The store boy turned towards Satish and nodded. Satish very reluctantly took out some cash from his shirt pocket and gave it to the store boy. The store boy came near the constable and gently and respectfully offered him the notes. The constable put the cash in his khaki pocket, "Tell Rajaraman I will come tomorrow. Your business is on a high these days." he seemed to utter while leaving.

Satish had been managing Maharaja Wines ever since the day he had got back home after taking the Mains in Delhi. Though Rajaraman naturally derided even this idea, he finally had to surrender as Satish had emerged the clean winner in their one-year deal. The results of the Mains were usually announced in the month of March. Just like Satish, all the other candidates were waiting for the Mains results that would decide if they had got the chance to get inside the UPSC main building for the personality test or not. They did not seem to have anything specific to prepare for till then. Their long, draining run had come to a temporary, grinding halt. Some of them were glued to the TV sets at their homes. Others caught up with their relatives and friends and girlfriends. Some of them wandered aimlessly. Most of them were just enjoying the home stay, movies and food. But all of them had to constantly face one set of questions from all corners: "Will you clear the exam this time? What are you doing these days? When are the results coming? Do you plan to look for a job?"

"Yeah.. I had taken her out last night. We were close during the college days… then ... She is here for some work now", Hardeep continued with excitement, "..for another two weeks!" "Quite interesting Harry..have a good time with *bhabhiji*!" Satish topped that with a chuckle that reached Hardeep on the other end of the telephone line exactly the same way. But strangely the pony tail and the orange kurta flashed in Satish's mind for a moment.

Ever since the moment Satish had come face to face with the balcony-girl in the Exam centre, he had been experiencing some strange feelings. He was not sure what it was – whether it was love or lust or crush or attraction or anything else. But whatever it was, the feeling gave Satish a kind of high. He often wondered, of all people why he should have come face to face with – her. However, he did not share this development with his buddy Hardeep, who had left Delhi on the very evening of Satish's psychology papers. "See you in March!" Hardeep had bid farewell to him. Satish was to leave Old Rajinder Nagar the following day. But that night in Old Rajinder Nagar was very strange one for Satish. He had the satisfaction and the relief of having completed the Mains. However, the predominant feeling he had was about – the balcony-girl. Hundreds of scenarios flashed in his mind. "Will I ever meet her again?" "What the hell!! Why is she not coming out on to the balcony today? Even the lights are off…Has she already left Delhi?...No!! Probably she has gone out for some movie..", "But of all people why did I meet only her?" "Is this love?" "Such a beauty! Gorgeous!...good girl!", "I hope I meet her before I leave." It was about 2:00 AM and Satish was still sitting near his window looking at the balcony in the opposite flat. He had smoked a dozen cigarettes in the meantime. But he had not taken liquor, not even a drop of beer. He wanted to be one hundred per cent alert that night. Every minute of waiting for her seemed like an era for Satish. It was strangely painful. Dogs barking at a distance and the solitary security whistle were giving company to Satish. The night was a bit chilly. Satish was going through the similar agony that he had gone through during his initial days in Old Rajinder Nagar. It was something inexplicable.

The digital timepiece showed 4:30 AM. Satish had fallen asleep by the window. 555 butts were lying all over the place. Satish's last day in Delhi before he packed up and left for home. He started packing up his books in a carton. He stuffed his bags and suitcase with clothes. But with every passing hour his frustration increased. He peeped out of the window frequently just to check if there was any sign of life on the relevant balcony. But he was not lucky enough.

No trace of the balcony-girl. "She has already left!!...But how was that possible? I was here the whole night.." The packing was over and it was nine in the night. Satish had his last packet of Senthil's Tamil dinner. He got his entire luggage out of his room. Before locking and leaving the place Satish quickly went into the room again; "Just in case!" But nothing had changed across the window. Leaving his heart in his room Satish left for New Delhi Railway station.

"Hellooo!! Hellooo!! Are you listening… you deaf bugger!", Hardeep's shout brought Satish back to the phone. "We are just having a good time… we are good friends..only..that's it!" Satish echoed, "That's it! That's it!" "Fool, who wants to commit with an unemployed soul.. I didn't even have enough money last night…managed somehow. In another two months…our Delhi prison life has to be resumed." Hardeep's tone mellowed. Satish jumped, "What resume?!" "What what resume?? What do you mean? You haven't filled the form? Did not see the notification? It had come on...4th December Employment News…also in all the newspapers. More vacancies this time…but have you not..?" Hardeep pounded Satish with a parade of sincere questions. "Dear, calm down. I had seen that… but that is it. Somehow I have even written Mains... that is enough. Even my dad is more than happy with this. And lots of stuff to do here...somehow I am fine.." "What?! Are you nuts?! Get the application form right away and appear in the 2001 Prelims… you have a real chance next year. You will make it!" Hardeep sounded desperate. "Why... you want me to be jobless for one more year?" Satish started in a sarcastic tone and continued convincingly, "I feel I have done enough... seen enough...whatever comes this time is fine... anyway Maharaja is here for me". "What..Maharaja? ...you have gone completely mad you fool..how can you even try to compare these two things..? Useless bugger.. you are very kiddish..think.. and is your father also okay with this?" "He is a gentleman...he has kept his word. He does not come to the shop these days.." Satish continued with great pride, "..I am in charge of everything now...Maharaja is going to be the best bar here very soon." "This is the limit you mad man! Hmm...I think you are afraid of the system...afraid of applying again and slogging it out...afraid that you cannot do anything." Satish cut it short, "Okay okay I am afraid of everything...so be it. I am anyways happy." Hardeep said in a hopeless voice, "I can't even believe this...see..think of those days when you landed in Delhi like a refugee... and look at the way you had blazed through and wrote the Mains. It does not happen even after many attempts for a number of people...you know that. For you things have just come your way. It is..probably destiny or luck..hmm..fate. Whatever it is." Satish cut short, "Socrates...please, please." "Allow me to complete you bastard...it means you are bound to make it big. So don't go away. Don't be so pathetic...I will talk to uncle." "Oh! Come on!" "At least start preparing for the interview...brush up your engineering subjects...optional papers, about Madurai...cultural aspects etc, your hobbies, national issues.." "Hobbies?!" "Yes, the Board asks you many questions on that. Prepare your hobby very well" Satish was now fully confused. He did not understand what his flat-mate referred by saying preparing his a hobby. "Yeah..you might have filled something in the Mains form…just recollect and start preparing those things." Satish went totally off on hearing that. He did not even remember what he had filled up in that column. "These are anyway useless things", he remembered telling his father while quickly filling the form. Was it watching movies? Playing cricket? Travelling? Playing guitar? Birdwatching? Collecting stamps and coins? "Helloooo…are you there? At least do this for my sake" "Oh..okay, sure..yeah Harry."

An uneasy calm prevailed among the candidates who had taken the Mains. Holi had come and gone and the Mains results were expected to be out any time. As usual there was no fixed date for the results to be announced. The candidates found themselves trapped in the quagmire of gossips and rumours. *Its now! Its then!* That was a part of the daily routine for all these candidates. Almost all of them who were eligible to appear in the Prelims 2001 had applied for the exam. It was scheduled for May 13th, 2001. Delhi summer was silently creeping in. Hardeep was back in his pigeon hole in Old Rajinder Nagar. He tried to brush up his optional subject and topics from mechanical engineering. He spent considerable time singing and listening to songs. But just like hundreds of other candidates he too felt his mind was too full of so many things that it was not able to handle any one thing that he wished to focus "I don't want to continue in this hell after May… For one more year!"

Rao's table was covered with dozens of magazines and four dailies. The coaching classes for the oncoming Prelims were almost over and the mood was set for the interview coaching. AIC was getting tens of phone calls every day. "The classes start the day after the results are out. There will be three mock interviews. 3500 rupees." "When is the result coming out?" "Expected to be out in two days…latest by this weekend. Interviews start on April 2."

"Even his father was not able to convince him. Strange boy… Forget it! How are you doing?", Rao asked Selvi. Mohit too was present in Rao's cabin at the AIC office. In fact, these days Mohit worked full time at AIC. Rao had asked him to be with him and help him out. Mohit had been mainly teaching current affairs but handled other subjects as well whenever needed. With the haunting clouds of the Mains results growing larger and darker, he had been asked to make the ground work for the interview classes. He visited the desk clerk at the UPSC regularly to glean pieces of information about the Mains results and the interview schedule. Occasionally he also posed as a curious candidate and called up a few other coaching centres to find out their fees, schedule, mock interview panel etc. After the work hours he had long chats with Rao before taking Selvi out for dinner. "Sir…I have revised the optional papers and in touch with current affairs etc. But it is overwhelming sir… I really don't know how I will be able to recollect all this during the interview." Rao was listening carefully. Mohit intervened, "Yes sir.. even I was very afraid while preparing for the interview." Selvi continued, "But the result has to come first. I am more worried about that…". "He is a fool sir…that fellow did not even apply for this Prelims. I too have told him many times. These days he is not even reachable on phone. He is in the shop most of the times. Waste!", Mohit brought Satish back into the discussion. "Yes sir! He tried calling many times." Selvi jumped in while looking at Mohit. Rao started after a pause and smile, "Firstly, do not feel frightened by the interview. Prepare well. Learn from Mohit.. he will tell you the areas you need to focus on. It is just a matter of impressing five people within 30 minutes. Nothing" Rao was interrupted by the knock on his door followed by Tinku with six glasses of *chai* in his hand. "Sir…I think the results are coming today…", Tinku said casually while keeping three glasses on the desk and smiled before leaving the room without waiting for anyone to react. Rao resumed, "I am sure you will clear the Mains..but nothing is certain about this Exam. Be positive and…bold. Prepare well. I still feel Mohit deserved a place in the top 10 last year..but life", Rao was interrupted again. This time by the phone. He picked it up.

"Oh…Okay…" Rao nodded, "Thank you", Rao was about keep the handset down when he quickly looked at Selvi, "What is your roll number?" "Sir..er!! .. sir..it is" Selvi was not able to continue. She felt as if her mouth was paralysed. She felt a huge lump in her throat. She started sweating in no time. She felt some strange, uneasy events taking place inside her stomach. Her heart too was about to explode. Rao got a little restless. The caller was on hold. Mohit quickly said, "004533 sir" "Can you please check this..the candidate is here.. yes.. yes..00…4533." Within two seconds Rao was given a reply. But in those two seconds Selvi died many times. And fortunately reborn. Her name was in the interview list. She had cleared the Mains. "Just one moment…please check this number also..hmm.. 141182" Rao said. He too seemed to start sweating. Mohit wondered who that candidate was. He was even jealous of that person whose roll number Rao knew by heart. He did not even remember Selvi's number...but this 14.. 11.. 82..is it..oh..okay..this is Satish! "Yes yes.. I am… hold..holding" Rao stammered. "Oh..really?! Sure?! Thank you very much!! That is just great..thank you very much!! Thank you!!" Rao hung the phone.

All the three shouted in joy. Satish's roll number was also in the list.

PART IX: CLIFFHANGER

"Okay dad… I will.. sure.. there is a mock interview tomorrow..ok..yes, yes, I will meet him now..sure. Bye..ok bye…this call is going to cost you a goldmine..Ok… I will call in the night from the PCO..bye.ok." Satish smiled at his new bulky, brand new Nokia 3310 before placing it in his trouser pocket. That mobile phone formed a part of Rajaraman's series of celebrations on Satish's success with the Mains. He had given out messages in the all the local dailies congratulating his son. However this time he had not announced any discount on liquor. Many of his friends had also placed messages in the local dailies. "Best wishes to our dear Collector, Desperado R.Satish IAS!", that quarter-page message was also seen in one of the dailies. Rajaraman was also very adamant on accompanying Satish to Delhi and be with him during the preparation for the interview. Satish had flatly refused that. He did not want to invite undue pressure at that stage. Finally the father had to give up. As a compromise formula Rajaraman had sent Kumar along with his son. Satish liked it.

Satish and Kumar walked towards the auto rickshaw waiting near the Old Rajinder Nagar Mother Diary outlet. "*Vigyan Bhavan bhaiya..*Maulana Azad Road.." The auto rickshaw picked speed. Satish took out a cigarette from his shirt pocket. He borrowed the match box from the rickshaw driver and was about to light it, when Kumar started, "I do not believe this!" "Come on! Don't tell me...I never vowed to quit this." Satish quipped showing the cigarette. "Bugger! I meant...can you believe you are actually going to appear in the IAS interview?! We.. you ..we are ..were...totally useless people and now...in a matter of ten days you will be in the UPSC building!" Kumar did not know how to express what he wished to tell his dearest friend. "Five great men... academicians..officers..er..intellectuals will be interviewing you! I mean...come on!" Many thoughts right from their childhood days to the day of the Mains results appeared without any rules in his mind. When Satish had called him to convey the news, Kumar had almost fainted in sheer disbelief and shock. Only after a few moments he had burst in joy and rushed to Maharaja Wines where Satish was still attending to his business routine. Many other episodes from their college and school days came and went too fast for him to speak about any of them. The millennium party at CP also flashed in his mind. Kumar was torn between question marks and exclamatory marks. "Tell me..frankly..", he tried to continue, "..have you ever thought..at any point of time that you too will be appearing in the IAS interview?!" Satish was taking deep puffs. Only half of 555 was left. The auto rickshaw had crossed the Secretariat by then. "Come on…even for BE… you took five years!" Kumar added. Satish grinned; but appeared to be introspecting. "Somehow…I feel… I know…this month will also go well.. you are destined for something big." Kumar said in a soft voice and he too slipped into the introspective mode. The auto rickshaw stopped. The halt brought the duo back to the actual world. They were outside Vigyan Bhavan. "But..still I could not understand…why is it your father wants you to meet him?", Kumar paid for the rickshaw and they started walking towards the building. "Dad thinks it will be another inspiration for me.." Satish continued with some more energy, "..and probably he is right."

"That one…the Annex building." Satish said. The duo was at the gates of the building adjoining Vigyan Bhawan. The security at the gates did not bother to stop them. He was busy with his newspaper and *paan*. Kumar and Satish took a few steps in. An Amby with a red beacon went past them to stop at the entrance of the building. A peon was waiting there to open the door of the car. Someone got out and walked in. One more peon with piles of files also got down from the car and quickly followed him. The car moved to the parking area. Kumar and Satish moved closer to the entrance of the building. A huge bilingual board in blue and white welcomed them with the floor-wise list of offices functioning from the building. "Man! The whole country seems to be dependent on this one building!" Kumar exclaimed. "Even the Met Department is here..I hope it does not rain today", he continued. "That was a total PJ...let us get in", Satish said as they entered the building. "Third floor", Kumar said to the lift operator. Kumar gradually felt his heart beating louder. Satish too felt the same way. By the time the lift landed both of them on the third floor, pearls of sweat had covered their foreheads. "This way..", Satish said while looking to his right. Within a dozen steps in the corridor they had crossed a couple of notice boards and a few name plates. "I hope I don't mess up anything", Satish told Kumar in a muffled voice. "Hmm…" The sudden loud ring tone from Satish's mobile created a ruckus in the whole area. "Oh…sh…this thing..where", Satish groped before picking up the mobile phone and pressing the green button. "Yes dad!", he angrily uttered while trying to keep his voice low. "Have you reached?" "We are here pa..I will call you later" "Okay remember..Prof.Xavier of the Trichy College" "Okay..fine..bye" "He is always worried about something!" Satish quipped to Kumar while dropping the mobile back into his pocket. Now they were at the office of the Principal Scientific Adviser to the Government of India. The receptionist was engrossed in some scribbling. She did not notice them. Satish tried to get her attention by clearing his throat but to no avail. Kumar too tried the same. It produced the same result. "Madam…good morning", Satish said confidently. "Yes?", the lady raised her head and said. "We have an appointment with sir..I am Satish from Madurai…mr.. Dr…Prof.Xavier from Tamil Nadu..Trichy College..he." The receptionist cut him pointing to the nearby sofa set, "Please be seated…I will let you know" "Thank you madam." They were both seated. The AC operating at super cool was not enough to fight their sweat. Some time passed. Satish was engrossed with snakes in his cell-phone. Kumar was busy with the page 3 of Delhi Times. "Mr.Satish.. you can go in. Your appointment is for five minutes", the receptionist raised her voice and said. Both of them quickly wiped the sweat and got up.

They could not believe their eyes when they entered the cabin of the Principal Scientific Advisor to the Government of India. They shared a very strange and inexplicable feeling that they had not yet experienced in their lives. There was not much difference between how this person looked in newspapers and magazines and how he actually looked. But for Satish and Kumar the feeling was as if God had appeared in person in front of them. They did not and could not bat their eyelids. Their mouths were half-open. "Please come friends", the warm voice of the Principal Scientific Adviser, Dr.A.P.J.Abdul Kalam, welcomed them. "So which one of you is going to become an IAS officer?", Dr.APJ cheerfully asked taking a quick look at both of them. "Sir..him sir", Kumar pointed Satish. They took their seats. By then Satish had been totally mesmerised by the aura of the great person sitting in front of them. Satish had lost the sense of space and time. He was beyond the seventh heaven. Kumar uttered a few words from time to time.

"Best wishes...come again with a box of sweets... Always remember to put the country before you." Satish remembered only those words Dr.APJ had said to him before they left.

"Looks like okay", Mohit told Satish. They could see the sari-clad Selvi come out of the main block towards the UPSC main gate where the two were waiting for her. The mid-April sun was merciless. Some days back, the Personality Test, simply called the IAS interview, had started for all the selected candidates. "Yes...she had done well in her last mock..," Satish added. "It all depends on the Board...I had got a sadistic board...only because of that my score" Mohit stopped abruptly seeing Selvi coming out of the main gate. Satish felt relieved that he did not have to hear Mohit's sad story once again. The interviews were conducted by six Boards, each headed by a member of the UPSC. Every Board had four other members who ranged from academicians to activists to scientists to retired civil servants to artists etc. The candidates were marked on a score of 300. "How…how was it?" Mohit impatiently asked her, not caring for her gloomy face. Satish had left them alone for a while and was busy trying to get an autorickshaw. "Why don't you open your mouth..tell me…", Mohit held Selvi's hand. A few others were also seen waiting outside the gates for their friends or daughters who were appearing in the interviews. From time to time they went to the adjoining lane that was buzzing with tiny eateries serving fruit chats, aloo tikki, cigarettes, lassi and the like. Selvi did not raise her head. Mohit could see the tear drops bulging out of her eyes. "The rickshaw is waiting." Satish touched Mohit's shoulder gently. The two followed Satish as he went towards the rickshaw. "I should not have come here today." Satish told himself as he got into the rickshaw.

The moment the rickshaw started moving in the direction of Old Rajinder Nagar, Selvi burst out weeping. "Don't behave like a school girl…what happened?", Mohit asked Selvi. Their auto was rushing towards Old Rajinder Nagar. Mohit's words did not have any impact. Selvi continued with her weeping. Satish did not know what he was supposed to do. The fear of his impending interview two days later was also beginning to grow in him. "Do not worry… you will get a good score.." Satish said in a subdued voice. "It was that devil's Board..."

Selvi uttered in between her tears. "His aim was not to evaluate me…but to humiliate me." Mohit put his arm around her. Selvi continued with a lot of difficulty, "How the hell am I supposed to know everything?!"

Satish finally settled for the sky blue shirt, striped navy blue tie, and dark blue trousers. Kumar had tried in vain for the white shirt with the maroon tie. "I feel blue will bring me luck!", Satish had made the choice. Like most other candidates Satish too had a spent a considerable time shopping for the clothes he would wear for the interview. Kumar was also with him roaming the congested lanes of Karol Bagh as well surveying the trendy showrooms in Connaught Place. They had spent one full day trying to decide the clothes for the D-day. It appeared as if they were finalising the wedding attire for the groom. Even then the friends were not able to decide on one set of clothes for the interview; they had bought two sets just to keep the option open till the last moment. "Okay I shall get it ready." saying that Kumar went on to open the blue shirt box. Satish was sitting on the cot with some preparation notes scattered randomly over it. "Okay Mr.Satish, why do you want to become an IAS officer?" Kumar asked while pressing the new shirt. Satish was surprised by that sudden question.

Quickly realising it was their final practice session, Satish replied, "Sir, right from my school days my dream was to become an IAS officer. A few of the officers who had served in my district have really inspired me. . .and IAS offers me the power and responsibility to create a huge positive impact in society." and quickly suffixed it with ". . .sir". Kumar, tried hard to control his laughter and said, "Okay Mr.Satish. . .why is that your academic performance is not upto the mark and I see you have taken five years even to complete your engineering. . .". Satish replied as if he was sitting in front of the real interview Board, "Sir, as they say in psychology, one of my optional subjects, one's environment plays a major role in shaping one's performance and. . . it is not always that good intentions are translated into impressive results. It is only when all the surrounding and situational factors." "Cut that crap!" Kumar cut him abruptly and continued, "Fool.. come to the point and. . . remember what Rao sir told you yesterday. Do not try to bluff the board...often." He said the last word in a subdued tone. Satish smiled and nodded. He said, "Sir. . .yes sir I have not been able to show good performance during the school and college days. But I have constantly tried to improve myself." "Yes...this sounds better. Fix this. Don't mess it up with any other psychology story", Kumar gave the green signal. By now Kumar was getting the trousers ready. It was close to 11:30 AM. Satish's interview was slotted for the afternoon. Kumar had fixed up a taxi to take them to the Dholphur House at 12:30PM.

"Why did you choose psychology as one of your optional subject?"

"Sir…I have always been attracted by the human mind and behaviour. I took this chance to learn more about the way we think and do things."

"Do you think telekinesis is a real phenomenon or is it only pseudoscience?" Kumar asked taking help from some sheets of papers lying on the desk. Those sheets had the top fifty probable interview questions from geography and psychology.

"Okay.. I can handle it..ask something from geography", Satish said in a confident voice.

"Hmm…What is the relevance of Malthus curve to India...especially at this juncture when our population has crossed one billion?" Satish gave the answer he had prepared well over the time in the mock interviews. He sounded pretty good.

"Sometimes you talk as if you are blurting out your reply from memory…try to make it natural…every time," Kumar gave his expert advice.

"In your view what is the biggest minus point of our bureaucracy?" In the mean time there was a knock on the door. The cab driver had come to mark his attendance. It was 12:15PM. "Okay I can handle this…I will touch upon corruption and... the urge to wield control over others..red tapism etc etc", Satish said. He got down from the cot. In another couple of minutes they were ready to leave the room.

Satish made a quick call to his father. "Hello pa...we are about to start... yes.. yes.. sure... thank you pa.. see you soon." After ensuring that they had taken the necessary documents the two were ready to leave. "I am sure he will get selected this time." Satish commented while looking at the locked room of Hardeep. Hardeep's interview had got over in the first week itself and he had gone home for a short break, before he could come back and be ready for the impending Prelims 2001.

Satish had the same feeling of strangeness and fear he had experienced many years back when he had gone to the Madurai Collectorate. Now he was taking steps towards the lobby area of the Dholphur House. He could hear every single beat of his heart. A few other candidates were moving ahead of him. All of them were impeccably dressed. Most of them were in newly bought clothes. Women preferred sober saris to bright salwar suits. A few male candidates had come in dark blazers; the April sun fried their bodies; but they did not have the choice of attending the interview in winters. On reaching the reception area the candidates were asked to produce a few documents including the interview call letter. The clerks on duty verified the documents and let the candidates move on to the waiting hall. "Yes..here..thank you." Satish submitted his basic documents.

He was then made to go to the waiting hall. It was a big hall with high ceilings and an old chandelier. The afternoon session interviews were to begin at 2:30. Each Board would handle six candidates each session. One of the peons at the entrance of the waiting hall asked Satish for the interview admit card. On checking out something on it, he said, "Sit there." pointing to a set of six chairs placed on the right side of the room. Four of them were already occupied. The room had six such clusters of chairs corresponding to the interview boards where those candidates would be appearing. However, the candidates were not told which cluster corresponded to which Board. Satish took one of the two vacant seats in his group. He was not nervous; he was not calm either. The other four were apparently busy with the couple of newspapers kept there. Two of them were conversing occasionally. The other vacant chair was to Satish's left.

Within some time the sixth candidate too joined them. It was a woman. She was looking pretty in a sky blue cotton saree. The other four candidates lifted their heads simultaneously to see who it was. Satish did not bother initially. But in no time he too turned to have a look at the new candidate. But what Satish saw was something that he could not have imagined even in his wildest hallucinations. "This cannot be true!" His heart, which was already a bit uneasy, without waiting for anything more – just exploded. The woman in the cotton saree was none other than the balcony-girl.

Soon a peon came to their group and got some basic details filled in some sheet that already had their names in it. He brought Satish back to his senses. Satish remembered he was in the waiting hall of UPSC and would be appearing for the IAS interview very shortly. Satish's name was in the second position. He too filled the required details. But before returning the sheet back to the peon, he noticed the name Payal Khanna. It was the first name in the list. "Sir.. which Board is this?", the male candidate to the right of Satish asked the peon. With a mischievous smile the peon replied, "Don't know…will get to know soon" Most of the candidates felt their outcome in the interview depended largely on the interview Board they were allotted. While some Boards were considered to be generous with the scores, a few were dreaded by the candidates. "I hope it is not his Board.. he gave me only 65 marks last year…he will kick me out if he sees me this time too", Satish could hear one of them tell Payal. She seemed to be interested in a conversation and they both got involved in a round of revision of the dailies. Satish appeared as if he did not care about the interview. He could hear only his heart beat. Loud and clear. Occasionally some cryptic statistics, esoteric terminologies and street smart philosophies fell in his ears. He felt as if his striped tie suddenly got life and started strangulating him. Things were getting beyond his control. He was beginning to sweat. "Is it because of the IAS interview or this girl..Payal?", Satish wondered. He could not find an answer. "Cool down Satish…cool down", he told himself.

The peon came and told Payal something. Satish could not hear it properly. "Thank God...it is not his Board!", Payal gave a sigh of relief. All the others wished her good luck as she got up to move out of the waiting hall. Satish tried and looked at her; with much difficulty he too gave a casual smile and wished, "Good luck!" Payal smiled and thanked him. Her smile almost killed Satish.

Payal proceeded to the room where the concerned Board had assembled. "You follow her and wait outside the interview room", the peon told Satish. Satish felt a huge lump in his throat. He followed Payal. His heart went with her. The interview Board was waiting for him.

Satish was seated on the chair outside the interview room. Payal had gone inside the interview room a few minutes back. Satish was still in a state of riot; his tummy too had started troubling him. "It's going to take another 20 minutes minimum." Satish quickly walked across the corridor and entered the gents' washroom. After struggling with the flush and the soap solution he finally emerged out of the washroom successful. He started walking back towards his chair kept outside the interview hall. "Is this all happening for real? Am I actually going to be interviewed by the Board? It appears very peculiar, strange..surprising..foolish...how have I come all the way till this interview room! Am I worth all this..it is pure luck..divine... no it is just destiny..as Kumar says. From where did father get this crazy idea!...I wish he were here with me now! He is everything to me. . . Wait..who is that..dad! yeah..it is dad!" Satish was shell-shocked to see his father there right in front of him in the corridor. Satish just stood still in the middle of the corridor. He could not understand what was happening around him. He could not react. He was too stunned even to utter a word. "Any problem...are you okay? Which Board?", the father quickly turned into a peon and asked him. Satish tried to come to his senses, "Er. . . yes..okay sir.." and hurried towards his seat outside the interview room. His mind was playing tricks with him. 15 minutes had passed since Payal had gone in. "I hope it goes well for her. . . she should surely make it to IAS", Satish was telling himself.

The Chairman of the Board was seated at the centre with two members to each of his sides. There was a huge desk. The candidates sat facing the Chairman. All the members asked a few questions with the Chairman usually opening or closing the interview. "Will I really become an IAS officer? Is this whole Exam really the hare and tortoise race that Rao had talked about? What rubbish!! There are so many intelligent people like Mohit who have failed even after many attempts. But Harry will get in this time. He will surely make it!...Hardeep I.P.S." The door opened at that moment and Payal came out. Satish looked up, quite eager to get a quick feedback about the interview

Board; also just to catch a glimpse of her. But before even he could realise anything she rushed out and the sky blue saree disappeared.

Satish entered the interview room. "I hope they do not kill me."

After the initial pleasantries like "Did you have tea?", "Make yourself comfortable" etc, the Chairman opened the actual interview with some basics on Indian polity. Satish appeared to handle them comfortably. The Chairman then requested the member next to him to take over. It was a lady.

"What do think is the major problem with child labour?"

"Madam, it is the physical abuse of children. Tinku is…er..these children are not only deprived of a basic standard of life...education and proper shelter to sleep and lead a healthy life…but are also subjected to brutal forms of physical abuse". Satish paused for a while and continued, "Child labour should be banned and basic entitlement of food and education has to reach every child…as a matter of right." The member just nodded her head and asked, "Are you aware of any such laws existing in our country" "Sorry madam.. I am not aware" "Do you know the incidence of child labour in our neighbouring countries?" "Sorry madam.. I am not sure of that." The member continued with her questions. "How can you, as an individual, help out these children who are … subjected to this exploitation?"

"Madam..I think as an individual we should not tolerate any physical abuse of children in front of us..er.. there are provisions in law about this and… such abusers should be put behind the bars. The help of local police and other agencies needs to be taken." Satish was not sure what he was blurting out. But he seemed to be confident. The lady member nodded and gestured the adjoining member, who was a professor in the civil engineering department of REC, Hamirpur. He started.

The questions he had asked did not sound like any language known to Satish. Satish desperately tried to keep in sync with the questions and decipher what was being asked. But most of the terms even failed to enter his mind. He could only make out that the member was asking him something connected to engineering and technology. Soon he reminded himself what Kumar had told him just before seeing him off from the gates the Dolphur House, "You can get frightened; but do not show fear on your face." The member was getting impatient with every passing question and the corresponding "Sorry sir" answers. Finally he finished his turn with "I can only pity the education system of our country" and passed on the turn to the next member. Satish's feet stopped trembling on hearing that. His heartbeat mellowed down. He tried hard and even succeeded in giving a simple smile.

The third member opened, "Are you aware of the hierarchy and various levels in the IAS?" Satish stammered, "Sir…do you ..mean ..

sir first posting is sub collector then collector..". The member looked obviously disappointed and rephrased the question in an attempt to get the right answer, "I mean ..the levels like deputy secretary, joint secretary etc.. what is the hierarchy?" Satish had heard various designations like joint secretary, deputy secretary, chief secretary etc but was not sure which secretary came after whom. Rather than spoiling the show further he settled the matter with one more, "Sorry sir..I am not sure of that." "Okay", the member continued, "…if selected to IAS do you think you can bring about a change in the system?" "Sir.." Satish had a quick eye contact with everyone and said, "I can!" The member looked at him gesturing him to substantiate. Somehow Satish instantaneously started, "Sir..I do not claim that I will be changing the entire system overnight... For that matter no one sane can make that claim. It is like this sir.. once I was talking a walk in the beach, that had many starfishes washed ashore. At a distant I could see a little kid picking up one.." The entire Board was in rapt attention listening to this. Satish concluded his answer, "So..every little effort matters sir." The member who had asked that did not show any reaction on his face. The Chairman too toed the line of the member.

Kumar, who was waiting outside, had walked up and down the adjoining by-lane several times. A few glasses of *lassi* had gone down his throat. He was also done with a dozen cigarettes. Anxiety was engulfing him more and more with every passing minute. "I hope the whole stuff turns out well." The dangerous combination of the hot sun and dry wind also ensured that his mind could not be at ease.

"Mr.Satish", the fourth member of the Board started with a thumping voice, "your hobby is.. business development. Can you please tell us what it is about?" Instantaneously Satish felt as if someone had put a huge block of ice on his shoulders. Heavy and chill. His legs started trembling again. "Hobby!!! I never knew what I had filled. And this business development stuff!! What was it?! I should have paid attention to Harry's words." "Yes…" the member said looking at the huge wall clock and Satish's blank face. "Er..sir.."., Satish started with nothing in his mind. "..I believe… there is a great need for enterprise at all levels...whenever I find time I help out my father with his business and that is my hobby…business development." Looking understandably unconvinced, the member probed further, "Can you tell us more on what exactly you do?..what is the business and how you." Satish shot even before the member could complete the question, "Sir.. my father is running a wine..liquor shop in Madurai. He is in fact the number one in Madurai..I had always wanted to be attached with that. During my free time I hang out in the shop and help my father..but he never liked this." Unmindful of the reaction of the members Satish continued, "…in fact it was my first love sir. I wanted my shop..Maharaja Wines to be the standard for liquor shop and bar in the whole state..I worked a lot on modernising the shop..I had designed some emblems and logos for the shop..my friends really helped me…I had managed the shop for a few weeks…mm..even during the break after the Mains exam sir." The interview Board tried to come to terms with what they were listening, however they seemed to be interested in what Satish said. "Sir..the demand management..crowd management plays a very important part in this whole business. Especially during the days of..election rallies, new movie releases, festivals.. it really becomes a real problem. The rush is just…unimaginable! I had devised some techniques to ease this out..there are also other complexities like the local rowdies, police men, politicians, officers, NGOs..Managing the whole thing becomes a nightmare at times ..sir. But my father has the talent to do that…but he is totally against me ..even entering the shop.. he feels I should become.. I mean I should not do his business…sir." Satish concluded that quickly realising that his tongue had gone out of control. The Board was silent for a moment. Not knowing what was going on and what he was supposed to do, Satish, as if to break the silence, said in a feeble voice, "Sir." On hearing that, the Chairman quickly started, "Mr. Satish, why do you want to become an IAS officer?" The countless rehearsals Satish had done for answering the question came to his mind. Childhood dream. Officers inspiration. Impact. Responsibility. Society. Power. He started, "Sir..", he tried to remember what Kumar had told him that morning. "..sir… I truly believe IAS officers can make a great positive impact to the society. But during my school days I ...never had the even the slightest inclination towards this..in fact I hated it...I am…I was not fit for it." The Chairman gave a puzzled look. Satish took his eyes off from the Chairman and looking down continued in a soft tone, "But what I had seen in Orissa changed my life…" After uttering a few more sentences he stopped and looked up to the Chairman again. All the other members of the Board were silent.

"Okay Mr.Satish…thank you, all the best!" the Chairman said.

Satish stood up and thanked everyone before walking out of the interview hall.

"I will let you know *pa*…I will get a call…in any case it will be out before six", Satish told Rajaraman before seeing him off. Looking cool Satish was chatting with one of the customers while the store boy was taking out a chilled Kalyani Black Label.

9th May 2001. The results were expected to be out that day. Unable to handle his record anxiety Rajaraman had returned home around 3PM leaving affairs of Maharaja Wines to Satish. It was around 4:30 when the telephone rang. Satish picked it. The call was from Delhi, as Satish had expected.

May 11, 2011. IAS Exam results were announced. Ms.Divyadarshini, a law graduate from Tamil Nadu, emerged the all India topper. AIR 001.

The District Collector, East Godavari district, Andhra Pradesh, gave a call to the Collector of the adjoining Khammam district.

"I got a great news for you!! Any guesses?"

"Hmm.. should I call you back..?"

"Come on! Don't act pricey…"

"No, no…fool…the MLA is here."

"OK, You know what?! Ranks are out … out of the top ten, can you believe?!!…four are from Mohit's institute!"

"What?!!!... super!! Selvi called?"

"Mmm…she's in Delhi now for some Planning Commission stuff."

"Okay... I shall call you later… bye Payal."

"Bye! Wait…wait…are you coming this week? The children are missing you... even your father wants to see you…okay..bye".

Before resuming his meeting with the MLA, Shri.R.Satish I.A.S., District Collector, Khammam, quickly smsed the happy news to the Senior SP, Varanasi, Shri.Hardeep Singh I.P.S.